Portal

J. Edward

Chapter 1

"What? Wait, where am I?"

I look around and see nothing familiar. I *can* see that it is definitely not North Dakota: there are too many trees and green grass. My eyes soon find a man staring at me. "Who are you?" My voice sounds small and weak in the vast, open field.

The man moves closer to me. He is nothing much to look at: not handsome, but not ugly, in my opinion. With a gritty, dirty smile, he approaches me. I brace myself for what may possibly happen next. "Hello, Jack. My name is Gangus."

"Gangus?" The name sounds different, but he speaks English and appears to be human.

"Yes. This place is the forgotten planet Pluto, or, as we call it, Earth Two."

"So, we're on Pluto?" Pluto looks a lot more like Earth than I imagined as a kid.

"Yes, Pluto. I can explain. Let's walk while I explain. I'm sure it will be a lot to take in but hear me out."

Awkwardly, I keep step with this Gangus guy and listen to him speak. "Many years ago, this planet called me here. I was dying on Earth; I saw the light that everyone talks about, right before you die. I walked toward the light and, when I seemingly reached it, I was here."

My mouth hangs open in disbelief at what I am hearing. Shaking my head a little, I say, "Wait, wait, wait!" My mind can't seem to wrap around what I am hearing right now. I pause in my tracks. "You mean to tell me that I'm dead?"

"No and yes. On Earth, you are, but you were called, just like me, and walked through the portal." Gangus pauses and looks at me intently now. The look is actually slightly concerning and making me uncomfortable, and the fact that he knows my name is beyond creepy. But hey, I am alive, at least in some form.

"You did walk through a portal, Jack, right?"

"Um...bu-but...yeah, I guess I did. I don't really remember what happened. I was in North Dakota and now I'm here." I gesture around to, well, everything.

"Okay, let me explain. Let's sit here." He points at a flat boulder a few yards away from us. I climb up the rocky side and lie out on the surface.

Gangus turns toward me. "I walked through the portal and ended up here, completely alone. I started looking around and trying to figure out where I was, but couldn't."

This story already sounds fishy to me; I mean, how does someone just come here through a portal? Well, I guess I did. Unlike him, though, I am not the only one here. I glance around at the almost-unreal, beautiful landscape, with its emerald, flowing, grassy fields and trees as tall as giants. It was breathtaking; prettier than North Dakota, for sure.

"So, what happened next?"

Gangus chuckles and continues. "Nothing, really. I slept under a tree and ate from the vegetation already here. After a couple of days—"

I can't help myself; I feel like a little kid. "Wait, wait. The landscape was already flourishing when you arrived?"

"Yes. Let me finish, Jack."

"Okay, okay. Go ahead."

Gangus leans back slightly and sighs. "Like I was saying, after a couple of days, the portal re-opened, and in walked a beautiful woman named Annie."

Oh wow, so this is like an 'Adam and Eve'-type situation: the first man and woman on the planet. This story gets better and better. "A beautiful woman, huh? Where's mine?"

Gangus flashes an irritated look my way and sits up. "Anyway, me and Annie tried to figure out what was going on. Every couple of days, more and more people started coming through the portal in the same spot."

"Did they have questions like I do?"

"Absolutely. Honestly, I didn't have much to say at the time. Then, one day, a box appeared through the portal. It was from someone - or something - that called itself the 'Overseer'."

A box! Really? He didn't think that was suspicious? And I thought I was gullible, being a veteran from the countryside. Not just any countryside; North Dakota is more remote than most places. I stand up and pace a little, still listening.

"This letter in the box told us everything we needed to know. The box itself was full of tools, supplies, even seeds of every kind of food we were used to on Earth."

I pause and look at him. "I thought you said that you ate vegetation before this box arrived?"

"I did, but there weren't many edible things to sustain a large population of people. There were no animals here, either, that I saw. The box had baby animals frozen that, when thawed, grew rapidly and reproduced."

"Okay, that's enough, Gangus. All I am hearing now is *blah, blah, blah*. Can you just get to the fucking point already? I mean, I appreciate the long version, but I need answers."

Gangus taps his foot rapidly, rolls his neck, and looks me straight in the eye, like a parent ready to scold their child. "I will, Jack, but first, it is important that you understand the history and the mission."

Oh my god! There is a mission. I turn around to see if that portal is still open. Of course, it isn't. I am stuck here: dead on Earth and alive here, somehow. I need to sit. Unbelievable! "We have a mission? What the hell is going on? The only mission I have or will agree to is to get my life back on Earth. I've had enough of this bullshit!"

Gangus smirks and pats my leg. Moving further away from him, I shake my head in disgust. This is asinine. He doesn't seem taken aback by my moving away and keeps talking. "Jack, your life is eternally over on Earth. It has only just begun here on Pluto."

"Yeah, yeah, I know. I am dead but somehow alive." I shake my head. My head is beginning to throb. At least I didn't have a completely new environment to have to get accustomed to, along with everything else being thrown at me.

"Are you ready to listen to more?" Jack looks impatient; one eyebrow is lifted and sort of twitching.

"Sure. What choice do I have right now?"

"The message that we received from the Overseer was like what we are familiar with as a constitution: full of laws, freedoms, and liberties."

"Wait, come on! We are supposed to obey or follow laws from some unseen, maybe non-existent Overseer? That's ridiculous. I mean the Constitution wasn't presented in a box with no faces to associate with."

"Jack, listen. You are the final piece to the puzzle." I stop and look at him. His face is dead-serious. My shoulders sag in utter defeat; there really is no way back to my former life. Disappointment weighs me down and I feel exhausted.

"What is this mission about?"

"Slow down, Jack. We will get to that soon enough. When we received the letter with the laws, the people here and I decided to build homes, animal enclosures, and gardens."

"That was smart. I mean, so you're a farmer, and there is a big community of country folk. Can you just get to the fucking point already?"

His eyebrows furrow and his lips scowl. "I am trying, but you keep rudely interrupting me."

"Well, damn. I feel like I'm aging waiting for answers to questions."

"Okay, just listen. More and more people continued to arrive, and our city grew very large. Only 1 in 25,000 deaths on Earth came here until we had a population of 50,000. You are the last person that will ever come through the portal."

"Hmm. Interesting."

"See, Jack, we are from all walks of life, all summoned here to Pluto. There are men and women, no children. There are politicians, military, engineers, doctors, lawyers, athletes, actors, farmers, truck drivers, carpenters, and much more."

Now, this is a good little tidbit. I mean, at least if I get sick, a doctor exists. Maybe there is even a sports team to watch games.

What I am thinking? This won't be like home; I have no family and no friends.

"Jack. Listen, you are as important to this mission as I am. We are the first and the last ones."

"I guess that's somewhat interesting, if it's true, anyhow."

"Most of us that came here were underpaid or even discriminated against unjustly, so it only seems fit that we take over Earth. That is the mission."

"Finally, we arrive at the fucking point. And just how do you plan on doing that? You just said the portal is closed for good. How are you going to manage to get back to Earth?"

Now walking, Gangus continues to talk. "We have ships that can get to Earth in a week. Do you know why Earth stated that Pluto wasn't a planet anymore?"

Why the hell is this important? "Yeah, it was something about Pluto being too small: a star with no life known on it."

"Exactly. Those were lies. They knew that life existed here; they even knew that it was flourishing with life on it. You can do comparisons of pictures of Pluto in 1980 with how it looks now, almost three decades later. They know we are coming; they just don't know when."

"Okay. When is this supposed to happen?"

We reach a small, open area and pause. "As soon as the Overseer tells us." I don't know if it's the wind blowing through the open area or what, but my whole body is covered in chills.

"Oh, that guy again." I try to shake off how I feel, or at least try to convince him it's not freaking me out.

"I know this has been a lot to take in. We can continue tomorrow. Look up at that hill; your house is the one next to mine at the top."

I squint my eyes and strain to see the top of the hill, which is more like a small mountain. The house isn't anything special, but since it's just me, it doesn't really matter. I start toward the direction that Gangus pointed. I yell back to him, "Umm, okay. Guess I will see you tomorrow, Gangus."

Climbing the hill, I keep pondering this Overseer guy. Who is that, really? None of what Gangus has told me makes any fucking sense. Honestly, this is just a complete mess. I'm just a small-town boy from North Dakota that went off to war and returned to be a little ol' hunting guide. If they think that I will lead this army, they are fucking crazy.

I wipe my brow of a small bead of sweat forming as I crest the hill. I stand, staring at the house. It isn't old or big, just a quaint, little house built for one or two people at most. The wood was raw and reminded me of some kind of mountain-man shack.

I turn the knob and open the wooden door. It creaks a little as I step inside. I take in the small shack, walking around running my fingers across furniture. I think about what Gangus said. I was just a simple country boy. What could they possibly want with me? Maybe it's my military experience. If that is the case, they will be unhappy. I refuse to lead some army of people, of which I haven't even seen yet, into some battle against my planet.

"What the fuck!"

My voice echoes through the small space. Frustration settles into my stiff shoulders as I open cabinets and drawers in the kitchen and in both rooms. Nothing. There is absolutely nothing to be found that explains my overall purpose for being on this planet. I find a beer in the fridge, grab one, crack it, and plop onto the couch. The house was very generic and lacks any personal touches. I have a strange desire to change that.

After a few beers, I strut to the bedroom. It's literally just a room with a bed. I collapse, fully-clothed, and fall asleep. Hopefully by tomorrow that guy Gangus has some better answers.

Chapter 2

The sun peeks through the multiple eastern windows. The aroma of bacon wakes me quickly. My nostrils are tantalized as my stomach aches from hunger. For a brief moment, I forget that I am on planet Pluto. I stretch and swing off the bed. I wander into the kitchen. My whole body shakes as I see it isn't my sister, and that's when it all comes back to me. I am dead, or alive, or whatever the fuck. I am here.

"Um, good morning, Gangus."

Gangus turns slightly as he flips the bacon. "Good morning."

"What the hell are you doing in my house?"

Gangus chuckles. He switches the burner off and lays the bacon on plates with toast. He moves to the table with the plates and sits. I follow, wondering if he is going to answer my question. If this guy thinks that he owns me just because I happened to show up here...

"Here we have an open-door policy. We visit each other and don't lock our doors."

"Hmm. Well, not sure I like this. So, is this real bacon?"

"Yes."

I grab a piece and shovel it into my mouth. I savagely finish my plate in a matter of minutes. I drink the orange juice sitting next to my plate. "I can get use to the bacon and beer; they're my favorites. It's actually the first fucking thing that I do like so far."

"This place is amazing, and you will see that more and more. The open-door is a trust thing that we do here, which is an environment we want to remain. It is different than Earth One." He takes a piece of bacon from his plate and crunches it between his teeth. "Now, Jack, we must continue on our conversation from yesterday."

I roll my eyes. "More nonsensical bullshit? Fine, Gangus."

Gangus looks at me with a harsh scowl. "It's not nonsensical. I know it's boring, but we need to be on the same page, have the same vision, dream the same dream. That's why it's important to understand the history of this place. It will help you to accept the mission to Earth."

Gangus finishes his bacon and orange juice. "See, Jack, I was a bodyguard to one of the best US presidents. I was actually shot in the line of duty, you know. It was an assassination attempt, March 30th, 1981. It was reported that nobody was killed. The president had been hit, but not killed. As I watched the president crawl back to his car, bleeding and in pain, I saw the light that you saw when you

14

came, too. The United States government covered my death up and acted as though I never existed."

My mouth hangs open. "Hold up a minute, Gangus. This just sounds like some sort of vendetta against the government. I will not go against my flag and my country. I shed blood for that country in the Middle East! How dare y—"

"Let me stop you there, Jack," Gangus interrupts. "Could I ask you a few questions about your service?"

I nod. "I guess; you're not going to change my mind about this, though."

Gangus continues. "What happened to you out there?"

"Well, the biggest thing is my leg. There was a battle, and after I killed a few guys, I stepped on a land mine. Damn thing blew my fucking leg into pieces. After getting back to base and getting medical attention, I was sent home on honorable discharge. I received the Purple Heart for my service and injury. I ended up getting a carbon-fiber leg and going to rehab at the VA hospital."

"Then what?" Gangus scoffs. "Forgotten about, right? You went back to North Dakota as a war hero, feeling depressed, sorry for yourself, like you deserved better; you fought, you killed, you were brutally injured. You made it out pretty good though: a successful hunting guide, correct?"

"Well, yeah, I guess you could say that." I don't understand what that has to do with anything. There aren't animals to hunt here, anyway.

"And that's why you're here, Jack. You're a hunter with a strong will and mind to help me carry out this mission as my right-hand man. See, like I said, it's not just you and I with a purpose; everyone here has some type of story of how their government did them wrong or forgot them. Basically, we are an army of the forgotten."

For some reason, this infuriates me. "No, Gangus! I don't see it that way. I chose to fight for my country. I wasn't forgotten; they gave me my leg back and took care of me. You sound like one of those conspiracy theorists I hated so much."

Gangus smiles. "Well, let me open your mind and tell you why everyone *else* is here. You need to go around, meet people, and hear their stories. Then, and only then, if you still feel the same way, it will be obvious that the Overseer made a mistake bringing you here. Go, Jack, on this journey to hear their stories. Discover why they are here. There are many like you that have gone on this same journey. Go, and report back to me when you change your mind."

Lot of confidence in that last statement! "Well, Gangus, what if I don't do what you say? I don't want to hear these fucking stories. You can't kill me for it; we're immortal, right? Fuck you, fuck these people, and fuck this planet.

Gangus laughs loudly and smacks me on the back. "You only become immortal once you believe in the mission. To answer your question, Jack, I can kill you, and so can the Overseer. Ask yourself this: do you want to leave all of this? Your second chance on life, where you will become important and receive the honor and respect you deserve. Just consider it, Jack.

"I will leave you be now; you have a lot to think about and many stories to hear. Go into this with an open mind and heart, Jack." Gangus shuts the front door, leaving me alone, his words echoing in my head. I hate that it's actually getting to me.

I sit on the couch, surprised, angry, disbelieving. There are so many emotions, and not knowing what to do about them, I do the only thing that makes sense: I grab a beer and go to sleep.

I wake up, this time without the smell of bacon throughout the house. I must be alone. I cook my own breakfast this morning: toast with jelly, scrambled eggs, and orange juice. I look through the cabinets, wondering if there is any alcohol on this stupid planet. I find a flask and a bottle of whiskey. "Perfect," I mutter to myself. I'm going to need this if I'm actually going to get through a day of bullshit stories.

I walk out of the house and down the hill. There is another house here, so I might as well start with this one. I knock on the door and hear a lady's voice. "Come in!" she says with a thick Irish accent.

I open the door slowly; I have no idea what to expect. Gangus is the only person I've seen on this planet so far. As far as I know, there could be life on other planets, and this person could be some alien creature. I brace for the most unexpected thing.

Surprisingly, a gorgeous, red-haired, blue-eyed woman walks in to meet him. She has a beautiful hourglass figure and luscious, milky-white skin. She looks to be in her mid-thirties. She speaks, and I'm so enamored in her appearance, I jump a little bit, startled.

"Hello, my name is Annie. Come sit down, Jack."

"Well, hello," I say, taking a seat on the bright green, overstuffed futon. "You're not exactly what I expected. You are gorgeous!"

Annie blushes and giggles. "Thank you, Jack. What exactly were you expecting? Some hideous swamp donkey?" We both laugh.

"Well, no, not exactly. Maybe an alien creature, though. Definitely not somebody so breathtaking. It's a nice sur—wait, how do you know my name? I haven't introduced myself. Are you some kind of witch or something? Can you transform from this beautiful woman to some evil, old hag? Did Gangus put you up to this to change my mind?"

Annie laughs harder at this notion. "No, Jack, nothing li—"

"Again with my fucking name! How do you know my name?"

"Relax! Gangus figured you would stop by today, so he told me to be awaiting your arrival. See, we have all been waiting for you. We all know your name and your story. You are the chosen one, Jack; the one we have all been waiting for. You need to relax and remember that no one here is your enemy. We are all here for the same reasons. Gangus told me you were not on board with the rest of us. Is that true, Jack?"

I feel a little foolish for my meltdown. "I apologize. It's nice to meet you, Annie. I remember Gangus mentioning you by name. He said you were the second person here. And yes, I'm still unsure about all of this. Gangus said I needed to go around and hear different stories, so here I am." I grab my flask and take a long sip of whiskey. Much better.

Annie eyes the flask in my hand and smirks at me. "You're right. I was the second person here, but my story goes back hundreds of years. See, after I died on Earth, I just floated in limbo for years. That is, until Gangus got here to Pluto. Gangus is also a chosen one by the Overseer, just like you. The rest of us, well, we are here because of what happened to us during our lives."

I nod at her. "Okay, beautiful Annie, what's your story?"

Annie looks down at the floor solemnly. "Like I said, I died much earlier than Gangus did. It was 1848, during the Irish potato famine. The potato blight was in full effect. My family was a large potato-farming family. The government said they didn't know what caused it, but we all knew: it was the government poisoning the water supply that we used for watering fields and even as drinking water.

"I couldn't afford to go to America like many others did. My mum and dad had already died; I was there to run it alone. So, with piss and vinegar running in my veins, I refused to give in. I was slowly starving to death. Myself, like so many others, wouldn't give up to the English government, who was trying to get rid of us by pushing us out to Ireland. Slowly, they got rid of almost a quarter of our population, myself included. I died of starvation. They wouldn't help us. They took everything I had and left me to rot.

"So, now I'm here; I fully support Gangus, and I hope you will as well."

I am shocked. I shake my head. "Wow, Annie. That's truly fucked up. I'm so sorry to hear what happened to you and your family." I take another sip from my flask and offer it to her. She accepts. "Can I ask you a question?"

Annie takes a long chug from the flask and wipes her mouth. "Of course, Jack. Ask me anything."

"If you starved to death, why aren't you just skin and bones?"

Annie smiles and giggles. "Well, see, once you believe in the mission and are on track with it, all your hardships, injuries, and hurt from your previous life disappears. You become the healthiest version of yourself." She gestures down at her body: full, healthy, beautiful, vivacious, not at all the starved, skeletal version she described.

My eyes pop wide open. I take another sip from the flask and wipe my lip with my arm. "Holy fucking shit, are you serious? I would get my leg back? I wouldn't need this stupid prosthetic?"

"Yes, Jack, you would, but only when you truly believe and when the Overseer agrees that you believe in the mission."

I contemplate that for a minute. "When do I get to meet this Overseer," I do air quotes around the ridiculous name, "and let him know when I'm ready?"

Annie laughs. Her laugh sounds like chimes in an echo chamber. "Nobody, not even Gangus, has met the Overseer, Jack."

I hang my head. This is starting to sound like a scam, the product of Gangus and his initial loneliness on Pluto. "So he's just a myth, a made-up figment of Gangus' imagination? What, do you guys use it to brainwash the rest of these people?"

"No! No, it's nothing li—"

"Enough!" I shout over her. "That's enough, Annie. I don't want to hear any more bullshit, made-up stories from you. I'm leaving; I think I should probably find out if there are really other people here. Goodbye, Annie." I walk through the door.

As I shut the door, I mumble to myself, "I hope she's telling the truth; she is truly beautiful." Annie must have heard me, because she starts giggling.

She yells through the door, "Good luck on you journey, Jack!" I drink another sip of whiskey, almost toasting to the notion.

I continue down the cobblestone pathway, or driveway, I guess. Are there cars here? Are there other people here? I haven't noticed anyone else at all. I guess there's only one way to find out. I get to the next home, walk up to the front door, and knock. This house is different than mine: it's got stucco exterior, clay roof tiles, and beautiful, stained-glass windows all along the outside of the house. It's breathtaking.

I hear a voice say, "Come in." I open the heavy, wooden door and walk inside. I quickly realize that there *are* more than just Gangus, Annie, and myself here, as a young woman of Chinese descent enters the room. She seems to be in her mid-twenties.

"Hello, hello!" she greets. "Please, come sit down. My name is Ya. You must be Jack."

I, again, am surprised that she knows my name. I assume it's like it was with Annie: Gangus must have let her know I was coming. "Yes, nice to meet you, Ya. I assume you know why I am here."

"Of course. You don't believe in the mission and are here to hear my story."

I sip on my flask and nod my head.

"Well, my story begins in 1982. China had a 'one child per family' law. I was 28 years old with one child and another on the way. The government told us we could only have one. It's not right, telling us how many children we could have. We were very financially well off and could easily afford another child. With the law, though, what could we do?"

I shake my head. Tears are forming and swelling up in my eyes. I take a swift taste of the whiskey; it's the last drop.

"Do you need a refill?" My eyes pop open, and I give her an awkward look while my flask is upturned. I nod my head and wipe my mouth. Ya fills my flask and hands it back to me. In the other hand, she has an ice-cold longneck beer. She hands it to me. She grabs a glass of wine and waves her hand in a silent toast.

"So, pregnant with our second child, I had to make a very hard decision: I could either have my child and keep it a secret, or I could have an abortion. I chose to risk it and have my baby. Long story short, they found out. I didn't want the repercussions of breaking the law, so I hung myself."

My tears aren't shy at this point; they stream down my face like two salty rivers. I stand up and walk over to Ya. I embrace her and say, "I'm so sorry for what you had to go through." Before she can reply, I run out the door, a sniffling, crying, sobbing mess. I head back home.

Throughout the next few days, I visit many more homes. I hear stories from so many people. Some were slaves, some were the last of their tribes, some were set up by their own governments as a scapegoat so the government wouldn't get in trouble. Some were lawyers that the judicial system was scared would do too much good. Some were political leaders that the government was scared wouldn't follow their corporate ways. The list goes on and on.

As I listen, I begin to realize that Gangus is telling the truth about this place. I decide I've heard enough and start on my way to Gangus' house.

I enter his house without knocking; I figured if he believes in the open-door policy, why not take advantage of it? "Gangus, you here?"

"I'm in the office. Come on back!"

I run back to the office, tears in my eyes, hate in my heart. I am full of emotion and stumbling over my words.

"Jack, relax. I can tell you're ready; no need to speak. I see it in your eyes and body language. You're ready, Jack! You're ready." Gangus' face is overcome with pride, like he has achieved a seemingly-unattainable goal.

I nod and smile at him. "Yes, I think I am." I wipe my eyes, but the tears keep coming. The stories from the last few days have been weighing on him since he first heard them.

"It's time, Jack."

"Time for what?"

"Time for you to take the oath and become immortal."

Chills cover my body, but I try not to show my excitement. "Do I finally get to meet this fucking Overseer everyone keeps talking about?"

Gangus chuckles. "Shh, Jack. Just follow me. We need to go to Annie's house and let her know you're ready."

Gangus and I leave the house to head to Annie's. As we walk out the door, I look up and see that everyone is standing outside. Annie is on the front porch, smiling at me.

"What is this? Why is everyone out here?"

A smirk crosses Gangus' face. "Well, they, like you, want to see and meet the Overseer!"

"Great, about time we meet this guy! Where is he?"

Gangus and Annie look at each other with shit-eating grins. They both look at me. "We're all looking at him. It's you, Jack. You're the Overseer."

My mouth and eyes both go wide. "Hold the fuck up. This can't be true. I didn't even believe until just now. This must be a mistake! I don't know anything about anything."

Gangus laughs, puts a hand on Jack's shoulder, and says, "You know more than you think. You listened, you learned from the people, cried with them, laughed with them, drank with them, hugged them. Jack, you are the people! It's time for you, Jack, the Overseer of the lost planet Pluto, Earth Two, to rise up against all evil, big and small, and take back what was once ours. Say something to your people, Jack!"

I look at Gangus, puzzled, still in shock. I clear my throat. "People of Pluto! I am as shocked as you that I, a small-town boy from North Dakota, am the Overseer of this absolutely stunning, amazing planet. I have heard many of your stories and they all still sadden me. We were all misunderstood, taken advantage of, and forgotten back on Earth, but here...Here, we are as one! As Gangus said, we are an army of the forgotten! We are one: one team, one leader, one army, one voice, one family. That's what we are: a family. I want everyone to have a say in what we do.

"If I haven't heard your story, please stop by and tell me. We will not be crying sad tears, but tears of joy when we make our way back to Earth and take out the evil of that planet. We can be 'the United Planets of the Milky Way' and take on every evil galaxy in existence. Do you agree?!"

With an overwhelming reaction of cheer, applause, and screams of victory, I now know my purpose on this planet.

Chapter 3

I wake up. Something feels different. I feel something I haven't felt in years. I look down, throw the covers from my body, and scream in excitement. My leg is back! I jump up out of bed and start singing and dancing. A few tears of joy escape from my eyes.

I run to Gangus' house and rush in the door. "Gangus! Gangus, you have to see this!"

Gangus enters the front room, rubbing his eyes. I must have woken him up. "What's going on, Jack?"

I kick him in the side of the leg with my new leg. "This! I got my leg back!"

He shouts in pain and eyes me angrily. Quickly, he recovers and pats me on the back. "Congratulations, Jack! I know that you're happy about that. Now, we need to figure out what the next steps are."

I remember my speech from the night before. "I think everyone should be here to voice their opinions."

"Jack, everyone is behind you and your decisions. The people are here to serve as an army and to follow the mission, wherever it goes."

I suddenly remember a story I heard from a middle-age black man named Cletus. He was a slave who was beaten to death on a Mississippi cotton plantation. I remember him saying, "I know we are here for this mission, but it feels the same as it did in Mississippi. Why can't we just forget about Earth and make Pluto our new home?" This story, out of so many, sticks in my mind the most.

"I think at least some of them would prefer peace," I say. "What we need is a great hall, something like an American football stadium, that will hold all of us. We could hold votes there."

Gangus shakes his head in disagreement but still goes to spread the word. The people of Pluto swiftly begin drafting plans for the new great hall.

I decide to visit Annie. We talk about Gangus and Cletus.

"Cletus' story is particularly horrible," Annie says.

"Did he ever mention to you that he would prefer to forget Earth and just live on Pluto?"

Annie's eyes go wide; she gets a strange look on her face. "Well, yes, he mentioned it, but we were told to—" Her face goes blood red and she abruptly stops speaking.

"Annie, you were told to what?"

"Nevermind, Jack, forget I said anything. Please."

I can see she is terrified of something because of what she brought up. "Annie, please tell me. Finish what you were saying."

"No, Jack! Not now. I just—I can't. I think it's time for you to go now. Bye, Jack." She damn near pushes me out of the door. I'm as confused as I was when I first arrived here. I don't understand what could have freaked Annie out so bad, or why she wouldn't finish what she was saying. I need fucking answers, but first, I need more alcohol.

I get back home and fill my flask with whiskey. At this point, I'm stumbling around a little bit, but it doesn't phase me. My body's confusion just matches my mind's. I grab a beer from the fridge, sit down, and think about everything from the last few days, trying to piece it all together. If I'm the Overseer, how did I write this scroll and deliver this huge box of supplies? This is the first time I've ever been to Pluto. And what the hell is going on with Annie not finishing her statement about Cletus?

Something isn't adding up here, and I have to fucking find out what's going on. I leave my house and realize there's a car outside. It's a beautiful, golden-champagne-colored, convertible; there are keys in the ignition. "Oh, nice!" I get inside and start traveling through the city. If everyone here lives in their own home, there should be 50,000 homes. I'm going to drive every road of this city and count the houses.

I spend hours on the roads, driving every block until I get to the last one. I count: 44,997, 44,998, 44,999, 45,000.

"How the fuck is it 5,000 short? This doesn't make sense." Gangus has some fucking explaining to do. What is he hiding?

I drive to Gangus' house, get out, and slam the car door. I walk in and hear Gangus talking to Annie. I switch into ninja stealth mode, tiptoe in, and listen to their conversation.

"Gangus, I almost let it slip!" I can barely make out Annie's voice.

"Let what slip?" Gangus asks.

"Jack brought up Cletus. He apparently told Jack that we should just forget Earth and live here on Pluto. Gangus, I almost let it slip about Tim."

I see Gangus roll his eyes. He takes a deep sigh. "Jesus, Annie, what were you thinking?"

"I didn't let it slip, Gangus! I said *almost* let it slip. I ended up just saying we were told not to talk about that idea."

Gangus moans in disbelief. "Why the hell would you even say that much? Fuck, Annie, now Jack is going to be suspicious about everything. Damn it! Annie, this isn't good, not fucking good at all."

I've heard enough. I tiptoe back out to my car and head to Cletus' house. I get there and knock on the door. "Cletus? You up?" I don't hear anything, so I walk inside. The house is in total disarray; there appears to have been some kind of struggle. Things are strewn around the house; there is broken glass everywhere. I'm very worried now. I look all through the house, but I don't find Cletus.

I decide to sleep on his couch, hoping he's just out somewhere and will wake me up if he comes in.

I wake up to the bright light of the sun in my eyes. It blinds me.

"Good morning, Jack. Why are you here?"

I jump; I didn't realize I wasn't alone. I rub my eyes. It's Gangus. "Shit, Gangus, maybe I should be asking you the same damn question."

"Well, I heard Cletus came up missing, so I rushed over here, only to find you sleeping here on the couch and no Cletus."

"Hold on," I reply. "Before you start writing checks your ass can't cash with those assumptions, I fucking heard the entire conversation between you and Annie last night. So, motherfucker, you have a lot of explaining to do. Who the hell is Tim? Why are there only 45,000 houses if there are supposedly 50,000 people? Why did you keep things from me? I trusted you, Gangus."

"Okay, okay, Jack. Let me explain." Gangus clears his throat.

"Yeah, you better start talking and make this all make sense, and fast."

"Let's go back to your place or mine; it's clearly not safe here anymore." Gangus gestures around the room at the wreckage. "They must have taken Cletus because of his dream of forgetting the mission and making this his home. That, and he knows too much."

"What? Knows too much about what? Gangus! What are you not telling me?" I am furious. I hate being kept in the dark.

"Let's go. I'll tell you everything when we get to my place."

I laugh dramatically. "Hell no! We're going to my place. I don't know that I can trust you now. I'm not going to your place."

"Fine, Jack, whatever you want. I'll meet you at your place."

"No. You ride with me, too." I head to my car, not looking back at him. I get in and put my seatbelt as the passenger door opens.

We get to my house, walk inside, and each crack open a beer. "Okay, Gangus. Start talking. I want the whole damn truth, right now."

"Okay, I'll tell you everything I know." Gangus takes a swig of his beer and belches. "Remember, please: I'm not your enemy. I just never thought we'd have to deal with the whole Tim thing, but, alas, here it is. The truth is, Jack, I

33

wasn't the first one here; Tim was. He wrote the scroll. He was the Overseer. I was the second person here. Everything was going great, until one day, Tim snapped. I don't know what made him do it, but it was just us here. He began fighting me.

"Tim said he wanted revenge on Earth. I was happy just living my second life here on Pluto. Tim argued that he was the first here and he would make sure that everyone who comes here will follow his laws, his dream: his mission, as he called it. That's when he wrote the scroll. He said there would be 50,000 people coming here. He claimed himself to be the Overseer and said that if the mission was not carried out the way he wanted, he would blow the planet up.

"Then, he cast some weird spell on the planet and said that anyone who comes here will be immortal and revert to their peak physical form. He said that he chooses who comes here and that the first 5,000 people would go with him to make the weapons and ships to take over Earth. That's what he did: most of the first 5,000 were nuclear engineers, physicists, scientists, and elite armed forces. He told me to tell everyone the story I told you: that I was the first, a chosen one, and that the last person to be a chosen one would be the Overseer.

"As time went on, I let *my* dream slip out to a few people, Annie and Cletus included, in hopes that we could overtake Tim and forget the mission. We wanted to live happily in our second lives on Pluto. We only wanted to deal with Earth if they fucked with us. But, with Tim as the Overseer, he held the power to blow us all up, so I carried out the scroll as he demanded. Now, I can't speak for everyone, but I know Cletus, Annie, and myself don't want to carry out this mission. And now, they probably have Cletus, in hopes that we will try to rescue him. If he captures us then, he will hold us all hostage so that no one else hears my dream."

"Wait, Gangus. Why not tell everyone and let them choose sides? We could outnumber Tim!"

"No, Jack. Tim is a very powerful warlock. He is crazy and won't hesitate to blow us all up. He has nothing to lose. As he said to me, we are all on *his* borrowed time on this planet."

"But Gangus, how will be blow the planet up? Are there explosives planted somewhere? How do you even know that he's a warlock? How do we know anything he's said is true?" I shake my head. He could just be manipulating everybody: all talk, no substance.

"I have no idea what Tim has been doing over on the other side of the planet. I've never been there," Gangus admits.

"Gangus, for fuck's sake! Stop being a chickenshit. Let's figure out how to overtake Tim and forget this whole mission to Earth. What is the worst that can happen? Tim could be who he says he is, blow us all up, and we die for the second time? That's a chance I'm willing to take. Are you with me? I'd hate to split this planet into even more teams, so are you in?"

"Oh, I'm in," Gangus replies. "We can't tell everyone just yet, though. We need to send a handful of good people to come with us and scope out what Tim really has going on. If we can do that, Jack, I'm with you."

I nod in agreement. We decide on a handful of trustworthy people to gather up and bring over in the morning. We picked these people based on their stories: Mike, an ex-Navy Seal; Tammy, ex-CIA; and Raul, ex-nuclear weapons specialist. "This group, along with you and I, should be able to figure out what's going on over there. Maybe, just maybe, we try and recover Cletus. It's falling into Tim's trap, but we shouldn't leave a man behind."

Gangus stands up and finishes his beer. "Sounds good, Jack. The whole Cletus thing will have to be determined based on the circumstances. I'll gather the group in the morning. See you then." He walks out the door, shutting it slowly behind him. I lock the door and grab a beer. Can Gangus be trusted? Is this some kind of trap?

I wait until I know Gangus is home and settled in bed. I want to go and talk with Annie about what I learned and the decision we came to. I head to her house and knock on her door. She doesn't answer, so I walk in. I find her asleep on her couch, half-naked, in nothing but her bra and panties. Her plump breasts spill out of her bra and the curves of her hips spill over her tight panties. I try not to look, but I can't help myself. She is so beautiful. I could get lost in her body.

At this point, I would feel awkward to wake her up. I don't want her to think I'm a pervert. Fuck it, this is more important than seeing Annie half-naked; it's not my fault she sleeps that way. This is about whether Gangus can be trusted. Annie knows him best. I tap her on the shoulder to try to wake her up. "Annie? Annie, wake up."

Annie jumps; I startled her, apparently badly. "Oh, oh God!" She tries to cover her nakedness, but her curvy body is too much for her two hands to cover. "Jack, what are you doing here? Sorry, let me grab some clothes. Wait here." Annie stands up and starts walking toward her bedroom. I can't help but stare at her ass as she walks away; it's got this hypnotizing jiggle to it.

It's too much for me. I walk up behind her and put my hand on her shoulder. I softly kiss the back of her neck. She lets out a deep sigh. "Jack, we shouldn't. I think you've got the wrong impression."

"Shh, Annie. What happens between us stays between us." I kiss her again; she doesn't argue. I start touching and kissing every inch of her body, front and back. I grab Annie and pin her up against the wall. With her legs draped over my shoulders and her back against the wall, I start licking and kissing between her legs.

"Yes, Jack! Oh, I'm about to—" Her legs start shaking; I go even faster.

"Do it, Annie! Make my beard a sloppy, wet mess." As she orgasms, she covers my face and beard with juices. I slowly let her down. Her legs are weak and shaking; she drops to her knees.

With the tip of my penis between her lips, she looks up and says, "I'll do anything you want, Daddy." That just turns me on even more. I shove my penis down her throat and explode into her mouth. She swallows all of it.

"Fuck," I laugh and shake my head. "I hope this doesn't make anything weird."

"Of course not, Jack. Hopefully next time we can have sex and not just oral," she says with a giggle.

"Absolutely! That was amazing, but that's not why I came here. Damn, though; I think we both needed that."

Still giggling, Annie says, "Well, why did you come here, then?"

"Gangus." This makes her laugh even harder. "He told me everything. You know him best; can I trust him?"

"Why do you still think you can't trust him, Jack? It was *his* dream to forget the mission to Earth and just live here, free and happy."

"Well, I know that now, but how do I know he's not setting me up and handing me over to Tim? I know too much, just like Cletus."

"Maybe you should sleep on it, Jack. Go with your gut feeling in the morning." She guides my head to lay on her voluptuous breasts. "Let's get some sleep."

I'm not ready to sleep; I am, however, ready for round two. I sit up on my knees, roll Annie over on her stomach, and start kissing her neck and back, running my fingers up and down her spine. I spank her ass and grab her under her chin. I tilt her head back and whisper in her ear, "I'm going to fuck you like no other man has." I feel her tense up.

Slowly, I slide myself inside of her, inch by inch. Each pump gets harder and harder. She's biting the pillow, but I can still hear her screaming, "Yes! Harder, deeper!" I continue to go, harder, deeper, faster, until I can't hold on any longer. I fill her full.

I roll over, give her a kiss, and get ready to fall asleep. She rolls over and falls to sleep; she is exhausted from all of that.

The next morning, Annie wakes up like a sex-crazed maniac. She rolls over and sees my morning wood. I wake up and hear her whisper, "Can't let that go to waste." She starts rubbing and stroking me. She kisses me and says, "Good morning, Daddy." She shifts and proceeds to climb onto my face. Her thighs are held tightly around my head as I pleasure her. She rides my face and starts stroking me faster.

She releases a fountain of wetness over my face. It turns me on so much, I finish like a bullet from a gun, all over Annie's ass and back. She moves so I can sit up and says, "Go on your adventure now. Be safe on the other side." She kisses me.

"Bye, Annie." I get dressed and get in her shower.

In the shower, I get the time to do some deeper thinking. How did Annie know I'm going to the other side? I didn't mention it to her, or did I? No. I didn't. Fuck, can I trust Annie? Now I don't know who I can trust. It seems everyone has secrets. I get dressed and run home.

Chapter 4

When I arrive home, I walk in to see Gangus, Mike, Tammy, and Raul waiting for me. "Good morning, Jack," Gangus says, smirking at me.

"Morning," I say, a little embarrassed. I hope they don't know I slept at Annie's, or with Annie, for that matter.

We start our conversation about the plan for the adventure. "None of us really knows what to expect," I say. "No one has been to the other side."

Mike, Tammy, and Raul all look at each other with a puzzled look on their faces. "What other side, Jack?" Mike asks. "What have you dragged us into?"

"Gangus, tell them what you told me yesterday," I say.

Gangus goes into his story about Tim. All three of them now not only look confused but a little scared of this adventure.

"So, let me get this straight," Tammy interjects. "You two assume that Tim took Cletus and is now holding him prisoner on the other side, and now you want the five of us to go up against 5,000 people? There is no way you can think this will work, Jack."

"No, Tammy. We are just going over there to stake it out. We need to find out what Tim really has going on. If we see an opening to save Cletus, we will take it."

"Now, this is the kind of shit I live for. Count me in," Mike, the ex-Navy Seal, says.

Raul seems more nervous, like he doesn't understand why he was chosen. "Why me?" he asks.

"Because, Raul, you will be able to see what kind of weapons we are up against," I explain.

"Understood, Jack," Raul responds, nodding his head. "Let me run home and grab guns and surveillance equipment."

"Great idea," I say. "Everyone, go home and grab what you think we will need. Meet back here in no more than two hours." Everyone leaves to grab what they need.

Gangus looks at me with a smirk. "So, are you going to tell me where you were last night, or should I start guessing?"

"No, Gangus. Mind your fucking business!"

Gangus laughs. "Well, I saw you this morning leaving Annie's house. I saw how you looked at her. You got laid, didn't you?"

"I said mind your damn business, Gangus! But, for your information, yes, I did. It was amazing. That's all I'm saying."

"Okay, enough said," Gangus says, laughing. "I don't need details; I know from experience how sweet that fruit is!"

This upsets me. I didn't think I'd be jealous. "Hold up, what? You mean to tell me you had sex with her, too? When was this?" I'm furious.

"Relax, Jack! It was a long time ago, back when it was just us here on this side. Nothing to worry about, Jack; those days have long passed." Gangus gives me a reassuring look.

I'm still a little upset over this, so I ask, "So who else has fucked her? Is she the town bike, giving everyone a ride?"

Gangus honestly looks offended. "No, Jack. Annie isn't like that. She's a sweet woman. You and I should be honored that we got our chance with her."

"Okay, okay, sorry, Gangus. I overreacted." I feel bad for what I said. "It's just...I think I love her."

Gangus smiles and slowly shakes his head. "I understand how she could have that effect on you, but right now, we need to focus on our adventure to the other side."

"You're right; let's not get sidetracked. You want a beer while we wait for everyone?"

Gangus laughs. "It's a little early for me, but what the hell. Why not? We can celebrate you getting your dick wet!" Gangus is hysterically laughing now. "Cheers, Jack!"

I nod and hold my beer up in response. I mumble under my breath, "My dick is totally bigger."

Gangus, still chugging his beer, chokes in laughter.

At that moment, the door swings open. Mike, Tammy, and Raul are back with a truck full of equipment. "You two ready?" Raul asks.

Gangus holds up his beer. "Not quite yet."

Mike holds his hands up in feigned offense. "What the hell? Y'all are drinking already. Where's mine?"

"In the fridge," I say, pointing toward the kitchen. "Help yourselves. We leave in an hour. Let's all have a few drinks. We don't know if we'll be able to have another after this adventure."

After hours of driving, we see the glow of lights ahead, so we pull over, shut the truck off, and set up shop. Mike pulls out his sniper rifle and ammo; Tammy get her drone and laptop; Raul taps into the drone's camera; and Jack and Gangus wait for the live feed of Tammy's drone.

As the drone flies under the radar, we see that Tim has a huge military force: thousands of airships, Raul says, with nuclear bombs attached. Raul also notices a new technological gun that he has never seen before. Tim's army is testing it; it looks as if one round of ammunition from this gun will split into hundreds of bullets, become heat-seeking, and freeze the targets when hit. There are tanks and jets with a seemingly-impenetrable force-field around them.

I've seen enough. "Okay, we now know he has a great army; let's look for Cletus!"

Tammy targets in on Cletus. She downloads a picture of him so the drone will only focus on anyone that resembles him and will only report a 99% positive match. We wait for hours and hours with no matches.

"Let's go back to my place and try and put these pieces together," I said. We all get in the truck and head back to my place. I am absolutely stunned by the info we got. I'm also still puzzled by what happened to Cletus. Where is he? Is there still a stone, or even stones, unturned? Something doesn't add up.

As we get closer to the city that everyone else is now calling "Immensity," I see bright lights, brighter than normal. As we get into town, we see this huge structure: my great hall has been completed! Above the doors, there is a sign that reads "Immensity Hall."

"Pull over!" I yell to Gangus. We all get out and look at this monstrosity of a building. I see Ya in the distance. I am damn near in tears and in awe on how fast the people built this.

"Why are you here?" I ask Ya.

"Well, you left so fast when you were at my place, I never got to check the great hall plans with you. I am the architect for this building; that's what my husband and I were in China. So, here, Jack. Here is your hall. I went ahead and named it, as you saw: Immensity Hall. I named the city while you were gone as well: Immensity. I hope you like it."

"Ya! Holy shit." I hug her tightly. "This is the greatest thing I have ever seen. We shall have the first meeting in it tomorrow afternoon. I have huge news to share with the people of Immensity."

Ya seems very happy that I approve of the building and its name. She is brought to tears. She says, "This structure is the same as the one my husband and I were working on when I took my own life."

I shake my head, looking over the building in awe and appreciation. "Okay, everyone, let's all get some sleep. We have a big day ahead of us tomorrow." I turn to Ya. "Ya, thank you so much. You did such an amazing, wonderful job. I couldn't have asked for more.

"Mike, Tammy, Raul, and Gangus, meet me at my place around 8 a.m. We need to go over our findings from today and present it to the people. Great job, everyone! My deepest thanks for your work."

As everyone parts ways for the night, I walk into my house, still puzzled about Cletus and Annie. I conclude that I can trust Gangus and the people of Immensity. What Gangus said about Tim was all true; now we need to figure out how to deal with him. I grab a beer and head to Annie's.

I arrive at Annie's place and walk in. "Hello? Annie, you here? You up?" I hear her talking, but she's not responding to me. I follow her voice to the next room, only to walk face-to-face into her.

"Hi, Jack, honey! I was hoping you would stop by tonight." She gives me a sultry look.

"Oh, really? Why's that?" I ask.

"Well, I missed you...and I'm extremely horny," Annie says with a giggle.

"I missed you, too, baby girl, but why didn't you tell me about your fling with Gangus?"

"What you mean, my fling with Gangus? Jack, what did he tell you?"

I'm a little upset at this point. Why is she pretending? "Well, Annie, he told me that you two fucked. Would have been great information to get from you so I wasn't caught so off-guard when he told me."

With an eyeroll and a smirk, Annie says, "You're mad about that? Jack, that was years ago, baby, and he is nowhere near as good as you. He didn't even make me cum with his five-minute session. The only reason we fucked is because he was literally the only person around. Forget about that, Jack. What's important now is you and I, okay? I promise you, I have no feelings for Gangus."

My face turns red in embarrassment. I don't understand why I'm even upset over something that happened years before I knew either one of them. "I'm sorry, Annie. I don't know why I even brought it up. I just wish you would have told me is all, I guess. No more secrets between us, okay, Annie?"

She smiles softly at me. "Of course. I'm sorry I didn't tell you; I didn't figure it was that big of a deal. But yes, I promise: no more secrets. Can I make it up to you with your dick deep down my throat or in my ass, maybe?" Annie asks.

"That sounds amazing," I moan as Annie drops to her knees. She pulls my pants down and starts licking the tip of my hard cock, slowly at first, taking each inch deeper and deeper down her throat until she reaches the end. Then, she starts to lick my balls, bobbing her head back and forth, until I explode a huge load of cum down Annie's throat.

Annie wipes her lips. "Thank you, Daddy."

Weak-kneed, I look at Annie. "Fuck, I think I love you."

Annie giggles. "Do you love me or the sex, Jack?"

"Don't get me wrong, the sex it amazing. I do love it, but I truly love you."

Annie blushes and giggles again. "Oh, thank god I'm not the only one that feels this. I love you, too, Jack, which is why we need to stop that asshole, Tim. Then we can be together forever, literally forever."

I give her a hug, grab her ass, and say, "We will, baby girl. We will be together forever and we *will* stop Tim. Gangus, Mike, Tammy, Raul, and I went on a scouting mission today to see what Tim really has going on over on the other side."

"Oh, wow! Really? What did you guys see?"

"Well, Gangus wasn't lying. Tim seems to have everything Gangus said he has: bombs, and lots of them; some crazy technological gun that has heat-seeking bullets that split and freeze the hit target; airships and tanks with force fields. He looks to be unbeatable. I don't know how this is going to end up."

"Wow, that sounds intense," replies Annie. "Any luck on finding Cletus?"

"No, none. We had the drone flying around for hours but it came up empty with no positive match."

"Aww that sucks, baby. I'm sorry; hopefully we can find him soon. I really like Cletus."

I mumble, "What, did you fuck him, too?"

"Excuse me?! What did you say?"

I shake my head. "Nothing, baby. I didn't say anything. I hope we find him, too."

Annie rolls her eyes. "Oh, by the way, did you happen to see the hall is done?"

I beam a flashy smile at her. I am like a kid on Christmas with this hall. "Yes! I stopped by to see it and talked to Ya. She oversaw the whole thing. She did such an amazing job. It's wonderful. We're having a city meeting tomorrow. I'm going to tell everyone about Tim."

"Jack...do you think that's such a good idea? I mean, what if nobody wants the same dream as us? What happens if the people still want to carry out the mission?"

"Well, Annie," I give her a reassuring squeeze on the shoulder, "that's a bridge we cross tomorrow. Let the people know the truth. Tell them the two options they have and let them decide what path they want to travel."

Annie shakes her head in agreement. "Okay, Daddy. I trust you and I'm here to support you in any direction you go."

"Thank you, baby girl. We should probably get some sleep now. We have a big day tomorrow."

With a pouty face, Annie says, "Fine, I guess that means you're not going to fuck me in the ass tonight."

"Not tonight, baby girl. Let's get some sleep."

I wake up to the sounds and smells of someone frying bacon and sausage. I wipe the sleep out of my eyes and start walking toward the kitchen. I find Annie cooking; she greets me with a kiss. "Big day today, huh?" Annie says.

"Yes, it is. Hopefully the people will accept this new information and side with us to reject the mission to—" As I talk, I notice Annie has pulled out three plates and filled them with sausage and big piles of bacon. "Wait, why are there three plates when it's just you and I? Are you expecting someone?"

Annie giggles. "No, silly, but I do have a surprise for you. Go look in the den."

I look around, surprised. I walk to the door of the den. Slowly opening it, I peek in. To my surprise, there lays Cletus, asleep. I scream. "Cletus! Holy fucking shit! Cletus, is that really you?"

Cletus wakes up. "Yes, Jack," he yawns. "It's me."

I gleefully give Cletus a hug. "Man, we looked everywhere for you. Where were you?"

Cletus says, "Annie told me last night about your scouting adventure. She also told me about what you're doing today, so let's get over to your place and meet with Gangus, Mike, Tammy, and Raul. We all make our way to my place.

They are already here waiting. They are all very excited to see Cletus walk in. "Cletus! Where were you? Are you okay?" They plaster Cletus with questions.

"Yes, I'm fine." Cletus laughs, a hearty, tickled laugh. "I was taken by some of Tim's men and they sent me back here to deliver a message."

"What message is that, Cletus?" I ask.

Cletus replies, "Tim knows that you guys were there, Jack. He knows of your plans. If you gather everyone into Immensity Hall and tell them about our idea not to follow the mission, then you, Jack, did all his work for him. He will kill everyone in the hall. There will be no survivors."

My face feels hot. My hands ball into fists. "Fuck, do you really think he'd do that? Now what do we do?" I say.

"Well, Jack, while I was held prisoner, I learned a few things about Tim!" Everyone gathers around to hear what Cletus has discovered about Tim.

"Go on, Cletus. You have everyone's attention," I say.

"Well, what I saw is yes, Tim has crazy technological weapons, and yes, he was here first, but why does that give him the right to control what we do here? Tim is no different than anyone here. He has no special powers as the Overseer; that's just all made-up bullshit to scare us all. He's not a warlock, as Gangus almost had us believe."

I interrupt Cletus. "Wait, Cletus, so what you're saying in Tim is just a man like you and I? No powers, only immortality like the rest of us."

"Then how did he know we were there scouting?"

"I have no idea, Jack, but he knows everything somehow. We might have spy in our presence." We all look around at each other. Could one of us be a spy?

Cletus continues. "The only thing Tim does have is the Bow of Unmortality, so he calls it. If he shoots an immortal person with an arrow from this bow, you die."

"That's it? A fucking bow?" I cackle. "How primal, so primitive, so fitting."

If Tim knows we were on the other side and about the meeting later today at Immensity Hall, there has to be a spy here. The only people who know all the details he knows are sitting in this room. "Alright, Gangus, Annie, Mike, Tammy, and Raul, which one of you is on Tim's fucking side?" I know it's not Cletus; he was held prisoner. Mike, Tammy, and Raul are all new to this, so it's not them. That leaves Gangus.

"Gangus, how fucking dare you? Why, Gangus? Why are you reporting back to Tim? I knew from the start you couldn't be trusted."

"Hey, hold up, Jack! Don't be assuming it was me. I'm the one that told you everything. It was *my* dream to stay here, remember?"

"Oh, oh, okay, Gangus. Well, it's between you and Annie. I know that it's not her; we had a long conversation about being honest with each other."

Gangus replies, "Before or after you fucked her?"

"Enough, Gangus! I'm going to hold you prisoner and postpone the meeting until I can get to the bottom of this all. I can't believe your back-stabbing ass. You're fucking dead to me, Gangus."

Cletus sheepishly says, "Jack, one more thing. While I was over on the other side, I happened to steal some of Tim's engineers' blueprints for some weapons they have."

I jump in the air and shout, "Fuck yes! Cletus, you're a damn genius! We can use his own weapons against his ass. We need to get ahold of this "Bow of Unmortality" and destroy it!"

"Well, that's a great idea, Jack," says Cletus, "but if you destroy the bow, we all die. That's the only thing that keeps us immortal."

"Okay, Cletus, so we won't destroy it, but lock it up tight so no one can ever get to it," I say.

Mike says, "So what do we do with Gangus in the meantime? And Jack, you and Annie are fucking? High five, bro!" He gives me a smirk. Annie turns red in embarrassment; she giggles and bites her lip.

I laugh and give him a funny look. "Not the time for that, Mike, but yes, we are. As far as Gangus is concerned. Mike, you're an ex-Navy Seal; he's under your surveillance. Tammy and Raul, take these blueprints, gather up a team, and start making these weapons ASAP."

Tammy and Raul both nod their heads in agreement. Tammy grabs the prints from Cletus and they hurry out the door. Mike handcuffs Gangus and escorts him out of the house. "I'm bringing him to my place, Jack. If you need me, you know where I live. Talk to you soon."

Gangus struggling and, attempting to squirm free, yells out to me. "You're making a huge fucking mistake, Jack! I'm not the informant! Please, Jack, you're blinded by pussy!"

I close the door and ask Cletus and Annie if they would like a drink. Cletus replies, "Abso-fucking-lutely! Beer me."

Annie replies, "I'll have a whiskey, Daddy!" I wink at Annie, grab her a whiskey, and get two beers for myself and Cletus.

"So, Cletus, is there anything else you can remember that we need to know about?"

"Nothing off the top of my head, Jack. Well, besides Tim mentioning something about coming to this side the day after the meeting."

I spit out my beer. "What?! Well, that's perfect; he will dig his own grave. The people don't know who he is, and with Gangus not able to tell him we postponed the meeting, he will come, tell the people the truth himself, and start an uproar. While he's here, a team will come with me over there and steal the bow. This is absolutely perfect! Cletus, are you willing to come with me to get the bow? You're the only one that has been on the inside."

Cletus nods quickly. "Of course, Jack. Anything I can do to help to maintain this perfect utopia!"

"Then it's settled, Cletus. You, Mike, and I will head for the other side tomorrow."

Annie asks, "But if you have Mike go with you, what about Gangus?"

"Tammy can handle watching him," I assure her. "Okay, everyone. I'm going to bed. See you in the morning." Annie and Cletus get up and walk to their homes.

Annie grabs Cletus and whispers, "Good job, Cletus. He believes everything!"

Cletus replies, "Yeah, but I feel so bad for lying to Jack, Annie. Poor Gangus is innocent."

"Shhh, it will all work out in the end, Cletus. This is the only way we both get what we want. Now go home and shut up. Don't tell anyone; remember what happens to you if you do."

Chapter 5

Today is the big day: we are stealing the Bow of Unmortality from Tim. I'm feeling scared and nervous; hopefully this is that gut feeling Annie talked about. I hear a knock on the door. "Come in!" I yell. I walk out of my room to greet Cletus and Mike.

"Good morning, Jack," they say.

"Good morning, fellas," I reply.

Mike looks around. With a smartass tone, he says, "What, no Annie?"

I laugh and shake my head.

He shrugs his shoulders. "I still can't believe you're fucking that hot-ass Irish chick."

"Well, believe it, Mike. We are in love and I plan on fucking her for eternity."

Cletus clears his throat. "Umm, so can we focus on going and getting this bow, fellas?"

I laugh at his obvious discomfort. "Yes, absolutely, that's what we need to be focusing on, please." I side-eye Mike and jab him with my elbow.

"Okay, okay," Mike says. "So, we know Tim is on his way here. We need to find an alternative route so we don't meet him on the road."

"Yes, great idea, Mike," Cletus says. "I know the back way; that's how I got back here."

Mike says, "Great, let's get going. I have the first three guns that Raul made last night; they're all replicas of the heat-seeking, bullet-splitting, frozen target gun. I'm calling it the HSF100."

"Alright, that's fantastic news!" I say. "Let's get going." The three of them get into the truck and start driving to the other side.

Meanwhile, Gangus pleads with Tammy to let him go. "Jack is mistaken! I'm not the bad guy," Gangus insists.

"I'm sorry, Gangus. I'm just doing what I'm told. All the clues lead back to you. If you ask me, Gangus, you are a very sick, twisted person. I mean, why would you make up this story about a perfect place to live and get people's hopes up about it? Only to go and tell Tim what our plans are! You're truly fucked in the head and need help."

Gangus laughs in disbelief. "Tammy, why do you think I would do that, honestly? It is my dream to live here on—"

Tammy interrupts, "Yeah, after you conjure Earth. Your story was good and very believable, but unfortunately for you and your teammate Tim, Jack saw through it. Now the people of Immensity shall know the truth. When Tim shows up, we will confront him with you. Everyone will see and understand that we don't need to follow this mission. We can just live life happily here. Jack will get the bow and more than likely shoot both you and Tim, Gangus, so your life is ticking away."

"Think what you want, Tammy. Yes, everyone will see the truth soon, only it's not what you just said." He gives Tammy a self-assured smirk.

Hours and hours pass with no sign of Tim coming to Immensity. Gangus is getting worried that his worst fear is about to happen. "Tammy, you have to let me go. Tim isn't coming, Tammy; he should have been here by now."

Tammy replies, "Yeah, okay, Gangus. Good try, but it's not happening."

Meanwhile, on the other side, Mike, Cletus, and I arrive in the truck. We need to continue on foot. We get out the truck and start walking. "How far is it from here, Cletus?" Mike asks.

"Well, I'm not exactly sure; my guess is maybe two to three miles. Tim's house is in the dead-center of his village. See, the people on this side don't have their own houses; they all live in three huge apartment buildings, constructed in the shape of a triangle. In the center of all of that is Tim's place. The other buildings are just big factories and storage buildings where the weapons are made. Some are storage buildings for weapons and vehicles."

I try to visualize the layout in my head. "Okay, so how do we get into Tim's place? I'm sure that's where the bow is."

"From what I remember, the apartment buildings have underground garages; from there, you can get on the ground level by Tim's place. In order to get in, you need to be able to open the garage doors."

Mike asks, "Well, how do we do that, Cletus? Is it a code? Fingerprint?"

Cletus chuckles. "I wish it were that simple. No, it's an eye scan, so we will need to either find a willing person to let us in or freeze someone and scan their eye. We need to do it fast enough that the scanner doesn't detect that the person is frozen. There are always two guards at each door. I noticed that Raul added an option on the guns—"

Mike excitedly interjects. "You mean the HSF100?!"

"Yeah, sure. Raul added an option on his version of the HSF100. You can choose either single bullet or split bullet. Jack, you and Mike are both great shots; switch to single bullet and fire at the same time when I give the signal. I will sneak down there, so when you shoot them, I will scan one of their eyes. Then, we all run to get down here and we are in. Then it's just a matter of getting to Tim's. As soon as you fire, switch back to split bullet; not sure what we may encounter once we're in the garage. Sound good?" We agree to Cletus' plan.

Cletus, with his deep, black skin, blends in with the night sky. He sneaks his way down towards the guards and stops about 25 to 30 feet away. He gives us the signal.

I look at Mike. "You better not miss your target. I'll take left; you take right."

Mike grins and chuckles. "Miss my target? Please, I never miss my target. On the count of 3."

We count together. "1...2...3!" They both pull their triggers at the same time. The guard on the right gets hit first; the guard on the left a half-second later. Cletus springs into action: running to the guards, he picks up the guard on the left and begins the eyes scan. Meanwhile, Mike and I run to the door.

Mike brags, "My guy fell first!"

I shot him with my middle finger and a glaring look. "My guy was further away." I laugh.

"If that's what you want to tell yourself, Jack." Mike bellows. "Good shooting, though."

They give each other a high five. We reach the door and enter the garage. There is nobody around; it's deathly quiet.

Cletus says, "Up these stairs, through that door up ahead, is how we get to the ground-level courtyard where Tim's house is."

"Tammy, soon it will be too late! If you want to see Jack, Mike, and Cletus return safely, you have to let me go. I'm their only hope. See, there is a little bit of the story I left out to protect myself." Gangus gives Tammy a sheepish, shameful look.

"What the hell are you talking about, Gangus?"

Gangus shakes his head defiantly. "Uncuff me, let me have a beer, and I will explain."

"Gangus, if I uncuff you and you run, then I'm at fault. I'm not willing to take that chance."

Meanwhile, on the other side, we have arrived in the courtyard; there's not a soul in sight.

Cletus looks around. "They all must be asleep or working. I'm not sure how many men Tim took with him to Immensity."

We slowly walk towards Tim's place. When we get about a hundred feet from his front door, we hear a loud alarm and a huge force field pops up out of the ground, trapping us inside. We are met by Tim, who comes walking out his front door.

"Welcome!" he says sarcastically. "I have been expecting you."

We are stunned. Mike and I aim at Tim with our HSF100.

Tim says, "Your guns are useless here as long as my force field is up, so you might as well drop them, boys." Of course, we don't believe him. Mike and I look at each other and pull the triggers, but to our surprise, nothing happened. Tim was telling the truth.

He laughs an evil laugh. "Told you," he brags.

I shake my head. I don't understand how he knows we were coming. "Bu-but how did you know? We have Gangus in custody!"

I hear a laugh, like chimes in an echo chamber, come from inside Tim's house.

Annie walks through the door, the Bow of Unmortality in her hand. "Looking for this, Jack?" My mouth is hanging open. "Jack, I want you to meet my real boyfriend, Tim." She hands the bow to Tim.

My whole body is shaking. "You...fucking...bitch! I can't fucking believe you did this to me! Why, Annie, why?" I say with a sad crackle in my voice.

Mike screams in frustration. "It's always about a woman! My fucking god, how did we not see this coming?"

Tim laughs. "Just so you guys know, this bow is as powerful as Gangus may or may not have told you." He draws back the bow, aims it at Cletus, and says, "Thanks for your part in this. You did well leading them here." He releases the red arrow straight at Cletus.

Mike yells out, "Cletus, no! Not on my watch!" He jumps in front of Cletus. The arrow strikes Mike in the mid-section. His body turn limps as he falls to the ground; his body starts to turn into a black cloud of smoke and vanishes, leaving nothing but the arrow.

"Mike, no! What the fuck, no! Cletus, what did Tim mean? 'You did well'? You're on his side?" I fill with emotions: anger, sadness, betrayal, heartbreak. I collapse to the ground.

Tim laughs. "I just wanted to show you the power of the bow. As you can see, I can still kill immortal men."

Annie walks down and picks up the arrow; it's now black. "As soon as you're done embarrassing yourself like a baby, Jack, you and Cletus come on in the house for a beer and the rest of the untold story I'm sure Gangus forgot to mention." Tim and Annie walk back into the house.

"I'm so sorry, Jack," Cletus whines. "It's not at all what you think. I was forced to do what I did. I'm so sorry."

I watch Cletus walk in the door. I reach deep for any last energy I have left inside of me, pick myself up off the ground, wipe my tears, and head into the house. I enter Tim's place. He greets me with a beer and tells me to have a seat.

Chapter 6

Tammy uncuffs Gangus and hands him a beer. At the same time, Gangus and Tim start tell the rest of the story: Gangus to Tammy, Tim to all of us.

Gangus begins, "The rest of the story goes like this. Tim was here for a few years before I was. He found this immortal 'Circle of Life', he called it; it was a circle, about five feet in diameter, made of a precious metal only found here on Pluto."

"It was what made the portal," Tim explains. "At the time, when I found it, I wasn't sure what it was, but figured it was valuable. I needed to wait. A few days after I found it, a large box came through the circle. It was a box of supplies."

"So, Tim started building a few days later, and then I came through," Gangus remembers. "I came through the circle, which opened into a portal. Tim and I were trying to figure out how to control the power of this circle. We both agreed on cutting it in half, each getting an equal half; but, after we cut it in half, people stopped coming through."

"Gangus and I waited and waited, until one day, we decided to put our pieces back together and see what happened. As soon as we did, the portal opened, and through it came Annie. That's why Annie was in limbo so long: she was on her way when Gangus and I cut the circle. So now that we knew we could control the circle, we split it again..."

"...and came to an agreement that, once a year, we would put the circle together and hold a draft, each of us picking 657 people, give or take, for 38 years, to make the 50,000 people of Pluto. In other words, all these people are chosen ones, hand-picked by either me or Tim. We both agreed that the first 5,000 would go with Tim to make weapons and ships for our travel back to Earth."

"I wanted to overtake Earth, while Gangus wanted to enjoy immortality here on Pluto. We also agreed that when I took my mission to Earth, win or lose, I would stay there, never to return. I agreed on keeping this a secret; we decided to never go to each other's side until it was time for my half to leave to Earth. We wrote this scroll as a smokescreen, so the people believed in something to work towards. They did, too, for many years, until Gangus slipped up and told Annie and Cletus about his dream to stay on Pluto. Then, Gangus made his last choice, Jack!"

"So now that we had drafted our 25,000 each, we split the circle for good. We both agreed never to put it back together. Tim ended up making a bow out of his half, the Bow of Unmortality, that could kill the immortals who do not follow the mission. I've never told anyone what I did with my half."

I look at Tim. My anger has turned to interest. "Wow, that's truly fucked up." I shake my head. "So, about this Cletus thing, you were going to kill him and told him he did good. Whose side is he on?"

Tim replies, "Ask him yourself. Mike saved him."

Cletus cries, "I'm on Gangus' side! I was never taken prisoner by Tim; I was held prisoner at Annie's house. She tied me up, told me what to say and do, and lead you here.

I nod; that makes sense in so many ways. "That would explain the night I came to her house and heard her talking to someone. Nobody was around, though; she met me at the door as I walked in.

Cletus says, "Now, if I may ask a question, Tim? I saw you shoot a red arrow at me, but when Annie picked up the same arrow, it was black. What happened?"

Tim chuckles. "Oh, very good, Cletus. See, when one of my red arrows kills an immortal, their soul is now trapped in the arrow."

I shake my head. "You are an evil fucking asshole, Tim, and you have the perfect, evil cunt with you as your girlfriend. You two are a match made in Hell!"

"So, Gangus, what *did* you do with your half of the circle?"

"No time to talk! You will find out soon enough what I did with my half," he says as he runs out the door.

"Guards," Tim shouts, "take Jack and Cletus away!"

"Wait, wait, wait!" I argue. "Tim, can I ask you one last question? Why set us up to be captured? Why me? Why Cletus?"

"Well, see, Jack, at first, it was just Gangus, Annie, and Cletus that knew of the dream, but then Cletus mentioned it to you. Then, Annie slipped up and got your mind wandering; then you told Mike, Tammy, and Raul. Now I understand why Gangus chose you: you, Jack, are a people person. People listen to you. You are truly the one that could bring the people together to believe in Gangus' dream. With Annie on my side, and you holding Gangus prisoner, the people of Immensity will all know not to trust anything he says. I mean, *you* imprisoned him, so he must be untrustworthy. And now, with you and Cletus in my prison, nobody will believe Tammy or Raul.

"See, Jack, in order to carry out my mission, I need all hands on deck. Gangus and I agreed that I'd take my 25,000 people and his 25,000 people would stay here; but now, after I kill you all, with nobody to tell Gangus' people about his dream, everyone else will fulfill my mission. I will rule both Earth and Pluto. Guards, take them away!"

Meanwhile, Gangus is driving to find everyone on the other side. Tammy runs to Raul and explains what Gangus had just told her. Raul, in utter shock, says, "So Gangus was never the bad guy? Shit. Where he is now?"

Tammy replies, "I don't know; he ran off towards his house."

"Let's go to Annie's; she has to hear this."

Raul and Tammy head to Annie's and go inside, but Annie isn't there. They're unsure of what to do now, so they head to Gangus', only to realize he's not home, either. They sit down and talk about what they should do.

"Maybe we tell the people the whole story, like Jack wanted to do," Tammy suggests.

Raul seems unsure. "I don't know, Tammy. Without any of them here, they probably just think we are crazy. I think we should take what we know and try to make new weapons, just in case Tim tries to come and invade us."

"No, Raul! That's just stupidity. If Tim and Gangus are both the Overseer, all Tim needs to do is tell the people it's time to carry out the mission to Earth. These unknowing lab rats will go to Earth, thinking that it's the Overseer's wish. Tim doesn't need to invade us, so we don't need weapons to go against him; we need the people to go against him! The people need to hear the truth. I'm going to call the people of Immensity to an emergency meeting at the hall."

Raul scoffs. "Okay, Tammy, you go ahead and do that, with no proof other than your words. I'll be at my shop trying to find what metal this Immortal Circle of Life is made of."

On the other side, Tim's guards drag Cletus and I to cells to be locked away until Tim decides to kill us, I guess. As we get to our cells, Cletus says, "Jack, I'm so sorry for what I did, but you've got to understand! I had no choice; you saw what happened to Mike when he got shot. I didn't want to die in my second life the same way I did in Mississippi as a slave! Of course, Annie didn't tell me Tim was going to shoot me either way. Now we know the full story, and you and I can figure something out to save us all from Tim."

I nod, knowingly. "I can understand. I don't agree with what you did, but I understand it. However, after what you did, most people wouldn't trust you, but if it wasn't for you, I would have never known of Gangus' dream. You were the one that sparked my curiosity, and for that, I thank you. But now we're fucking in jail, with what seems to be no way out. FUCK!"

Cletus smiles weakly. "Well, thank you, Jack, for understanding. I just still want to understand the arrows changing colors."

"Tim told you: Mike's soul is now trapped in the arrow."

"Yeah, but why? So, what, that means that Mike isn't truly dead. His soul is in the arrow, so how do we unleash it?"

I throw my hands up in frustration. "Fuck, I don't know. Tim never mentioned anything about that."

Cletus replies, "Exactly! He didn't tell us, which means that there must be a way. We need to get our hands on that arrow!"

"Yeah, Cletus, let's just ask that evil bitch Annie for it; that will go over well."

"Jack, remember the night you came to Annie's and you said you heard her talking but nobody was there? What you heard was her telling me to be quiet and that nothing is what it seems."

Chapter 7

Raul finds out that the metal that makes up the Immortal Circle of Life is palliridium. It is very lightweight, brittle, and a blueish-silver color. If broken, one side turns red as the other side turns blue, so you know which pieces go together, and regains the peak optimal strength as it was before it was broken.

Raul thinks to himself, "So that's how Tim and Gangus were able to take the circle and keep bonding it together. If Tim made a bow out of his half and can kill immortal people, then damn, I need to find more of this."

Raul is now on a mission to find more of this palliridium so he can research what type of weapons could be made to kill Tim. Raul searches the city for gold, silver, coal, and salt miners to help him explore in search of palliridium.

Tammy rings the emergency horn, alerting the people of Immensity to gather at the hall.

Gangus is at his destination on the other side: an old cave where he had hidden his half of the circle. He uncovers the entrance to the cave and enters slowly, trying to remember where he put it. "I know it's around here somewhere; I was just here not long ago!"

Gangus digs around frantically, trying to find his half. "Where the fuck did it go? I know it's around here. Oh, wait... what's that? Yes, yes, finally! Here it is. I got it!" Gangus says out loud to himself.

He exits the cave and enters the light. He realizes his piece has a red end and a blue end. "This is strange," he thinks to himself. "When Tim and I cut it in half, his half had two red ends and mine had two blue ends. What happened? Did that little piece I gave to Annie really make a difference? Could that have made one end turn red? I gave her that little piece so that if Tim found my piece, he couldn't put it together."

"Fuck!" he screams out loud. "Now I have to go to Annie's and hopefully she still has her piece."

He gets in his car and heads back toward Immensity to Annie's.

Raul found five miners and they go out in search for palliridium.

Tammy is at the hall, getting ready to tell the crowd of people of Immensity the whole story that Gangus told her. People are gathering quickly into the hall, feeling nervous but extremely excited at the same time.

On the other side, Tim and Annie are talking about what to do with Jack and Cletus.

"Tim, baby, can I ask more about the arrow that I picked up? You told Cletus that your red arrow turned black because it has Mike's soul in it, right?"

Tim nods and replies, "Yes, that's how I tell them apart. Black arrows have a trapped soul; red arrows are empty."

"Okay, what do you do with the black ones? What if you accidentally shot a black one at someone?"

Tim shrugs his shoulders. Well, I have never done that. I mean, Mike was the first person I shot with my bow, but it worked as I designed it to. See, Annie, baby, we are all immortal, therefore I nor anyone can technically kill us. I came up with the next-best thing: to capture the soul. To answer your question, if I shot a black arrow at someone, theoretically, what is supposed to happen is the two souls reverse roles. Say I shoot Cletus with Mike's arrow: Mike would be released and Cletus' soul would become captured.

"You know what? That gives me a great idea. I need to test if the arrow reversal really works; I will go and shoot Jack first thing in the morning with Mike's arrow. Thanks, Annie, for bringing this to my attention."

"You're welcome, my love," Annie says. "About time Jack gets what's coming to him."

On the other side Tammy is trying to explain what Gangus told her. The people of immensity aren't having it, though: they're booing and screaming, "Crazy lady!" People are getting up and leaving, shaking their heads, thinking this was a total waste of time.

Raul is out hunting for palliridium with no luck. He returns to Immensity and goes to Tammy's place. "Tammy, you up?"

As Raul walks in, he discovers an incredibly drunk Tammy.

"Why are you drunk, Tammy? Come sit down. What's going on?"

Tammy tells Raul about the meeting she tried to hold and how the people reacted just like Raul said they would. "Go ahead, Raul. Tell me you told me so." She looks down. Raul notices tears streaming down her face. It made her seem so human.

"No, Tammy, you tried, and that's what counts. The people will soon find out the truth."

Tammy asks Raul about his research.

"Oh, shit, Tammy, I've learned so much! The circle is made of palliridium. It's a blueish-silver metal and—"

He notices that Tammy's passed out cold. Raul picks her up, carries her to bed, covers her up, and brings her a pail in case she needs to throw up and can't make it to the toilet.

Raul chuckles and thinks to himself, "Well, we both had epic fails today. When is Jack coming back? Hopefully soon. I guess I'll just sleep here on Tammy's couch in case she needs help throughout the night."

Gangus get back to Immensity and pulls up to Annie's place, only to find she isn't there. Gangus heads over to Raul's place to find him gone, too. "Fuck, where is everyone?" Gangus says to himself.

Raul wakes up, knowing that Tammy will wake up with a hangover. Raul goes ahead and makes her his hangover remedy, Raul juice: apple, carrots, beets, and lemons blended together. He pours the mixture in a glass and goes in the room. Tammy is awake, moaning. She's wearing the clothes from last night, but her makeup is blurred across her face and her hair is sticking up. She says, "I'm never drinking again."

Raul gives Tammy the juice for her hangover. As Tammy takes a sip, she spits the juice out. "Oh my god, Raul, this is fucking gross. I think I'll deal with the hangover," she says with a giggle.

Raul smiles. "I know it's not the best-tasting thing, but it works; just drink it."

"Okay, since you went through the trouble of making it for me." She takes another small sip, swallowing it down with a disgusted look on her face. Now fully awake, she ask Raul why he's here.

"I came to check on you last night; you passed out, so I carried you to bed and slept on the couch in case you needed anything last night."

Tammy blushes. "That's so sweet. Thank you."

Gangus says, "Hello? Tammy, you home?"

"Yes, Gangus! I'll be out in a minute."

Raul walks out of the room. Gangus' eyes get wide.

Raul laughs. "No, no, Gangus. It's not what you're thinking."

Tammy gets up out of bed and steps into the empty pail. "Why is that here?" As she puts two and two together, she says, "Aww, Raul brought me a puke pail. He really is a sweetheart."

She walks out the room to talk with Gangus.

Gangus asks, "Have either of you seen Annie?"

"No" Tammy answers.

Raul shakes his head. "Why?"

"Well, there is just one more small piece of the story I forgot to mention..."

"Are you serious, Gangus?" Tammy shouts.

"Yes, nothing super-serious, but somewhat strange."

"How so?" Raul asks.

"Well, as I told you about the circle, I have half and Tim has half. I remember his half had red ends and mine had blue ends, but now, mine has one red end and one blue end. I broke off a small piece and gave it to Annie a while back, just in case Tim found it, he wouldn't be able to fit it together."

Raul replies, "Yes, Gangus. I found this out in my research: the metal is called palliridium, and I believe that the circle is all there is of it on this planet."

Gangus nods. "Yeah, I knew that, but I need to find Annie to get that piece back. See, Tim and I tried to make many weapons out of the circle, but nothing worked, obviously besides the bow. The piece I have now will not work for a bow, so I need to find Annie; it's our only hope to stop Tim.

"See, Tim's bow has red ends and only his bow can steal the soul of the person that is shot. However, my ends are blue; only my bow can reverse-soul exchange. Come on, I'll explain it on the way to Tim's."

On the other side, Tim and Annie are just waking up. "Well, baby, today is the day you kill that good-for-nothing Jack," says Annie.

"Yes, I'm going to take pleasure in it, too." Tim gets up, grabs his bow and arrows, and walks outside. "Guards, bring Jack out here."

The guards drag me outside of Tim's house, my hands and feet shackled. The guards chain me to a pole like an old junkyard dog. "Any last word from our hero that wasn't so heroic?" Tim laughs.

"Go fuck yourselves!" I spit at them both.

Tim draws the bow back, fitted with the black arrow of Mike's soul. He releases the arrow; it strikes me right in the chest but, strangely, bounces off me.

I start laughing hysterically. "Well, that didn't work out very well, now did it?"

Tim replies, "Shut your fucking mouth! Annie, give me a red arrow."

Annie hands Tim a red arrow and says, "With pleasure, baby."

Tim aggressively grabs the arrow from Annie, draws the bow back, and releases the red arrow. The arrow again hits me right in the chest; this time, it penetrates me. My body goes limp and, just like with Mike, I become a cloud of black smoke, then nothing.

The red arrow has turned black.

Tim lets out a sigh. "Well, that should take care of that. Now, we can carry out the mission to Earth, but now with everyone, not just my half."

Annie again walks down with a small tear running down her cheek. She picks up the arrow that holds my soul. "What happened with the reverse-soul exchange?"

Tim shrugs his shoulders. "I'm not sure, but we will definitely need to figure it out before we go to Earth. It doesn't really make any sense!"

Chapter 8

Gangus, Raul, and Tammy arrive on the other side. They see my truck but not the guys. Raul notices that the garage door is open and there are two guards down there, frozen.

Raul says, "Well, my guns must have worked; I see frozen guards down there. That's where they must have entered."

Gangus replies, "Yeah, but this was days ago. Why haven't they returned? Something must have gone wrong. For our sakes, I hope Annie is with them."

"Well, only one way to find out," Tammy says. "Let's go in there and find out."

Gangus, Tammy, and Raul walk in the garage slowly and walk up the stairs to the courtyard. They see Annie holding a black arrow, crying.

Gangus says, "Annie, what's wrong? What are you holding? Don't tell me that's what I think it is."

"Gangus," she says, "I'm sorry; it was never meant to go this far. I really did love him! I was just playing along with Tim's plan to be able to stop him."

"Where is Tim now, Annie?"

Annie replies, "I'm not sure; I think he went to work with his weapons development team because, Gangus, my plan backfired in my face. I had to sit here and witness the love of my life get shot down for no reason. This is all my fault." She sobs into her hands, clutching the arrow still.

"Okay, okay, Annie. Relax and explain what you're talking about."

"Okay, Gangus. It all started when Tim called me and told me his plans, so I followed along. First, I took Cletus prisoner in my house and told him the story to tell Jack so they would go to the other side. Then, I told him to tell Jack that Tim would come to Immensity. With you, Gangus, as Jack's prisoner, no one would believe your dream.

"Then, Jack and his team would go steal the Bow of Unmortality from Tim, only Tim never left; it was a trap to get Jack here, so that nobody would stay here. Everyone would go to Earth as planned, like the scroll says. I told Cletus that nothing is as it appears, but I guess that wasn't clear enough of a hint, and then everything got off-track. Tim meant to shoot Cletus, but Mike jumped in front of the arrow. That's when Tim told me about the arrow trapping Mike's soul and how the reverse-soul exchange happens, but when we tried to reverse Mike with Jack, the arrow bounced off him. Then Tim shot Jack with a red arrow, the arrow that I'm holding that's now black.

"See, Gangus, I wanted to steal Tim's bow and shoot him with Jack's arrow, but it doesn't work the way Tim said it's supposed to. Now, I've lost Jack forever."

Gangus replies, "Oh, Annie, I'm sorry you think that, but I promise you it will all be okay. Do you still have that piece of the circle I gave you?"

Annie sniffles and nods. "Of course, I do. Why?"

"It's a long story, but I need it back."

Annie replies, "Well, oh, okay. Let me go get it; it's in the house."

As Annie enters the house, Tammy yells, "Shut the door and chain it! Tim's coming with Cletus."

Tim approaches Gangus, Tammy, and Raul; he says, "Well, well, well. Hello, old friend. Never thought I'd see you on this side. You might as well just give up, Gangus. Your hero, Jack, is already gone. His buddy Mike is, as well. As for Cletus, well, Cletus was going to be next, but now, with your unplanned visit, maybe I'll shoot you next, Gangus."

Gangus yells, "Tammy, Raul! Run back to the car! Save yourselves."

As Tim draws back his bow and releases the red arrow, Gangus knows it's over. In a desperate attempt to save his own life, Gangus throws his piece of the circle through the top window of Tim's house. Just as he releases the piece, the arrow hits his rib cage. Just like Mike and I, Gangus's body goes limp as the red arrow turns black.

Annie hears the widow shatter and runs to see what happened. Gangus' piece of the circle is laying on the floor. Noticing the red end and blue end, she grabs her piece. It's the same way: one end is red, and the other is blue. Annie matches the colors together. The half circle is now bonded back together; it transforms into a bow.

Annie grabs the bow. She notices her bow has blue ends and Tim's bow ends are red. Annie takes my arrow, draws the bow back, and releases the arrow toward Tim. The arrow hits Tim in the upper shoulder and he drops slowly to the ground. He screams, "No! Why? Annie, why?!"

"Because I love *him*, Tim!" Tim's body goes limp and turns a purplish-colored smoke. He vanishes into the arrow. As the purple smoke enters the arrow, the arrow releases a black smoke. Once the smoke clears, there I lay.

Annie falls to the floor, crying hysterically. Cletus rushes up to me. "Jack, is it really you?"

I smile up at him. "Yes, Cletus, it's really me. What did I miss?"

Cletus explains everything and how Annie shot Tim.

"And Gangus?" I look around. "Where is Gangus?"

Cletus picks up the arrow and shows it to me. "Right here, Jack. He sacrificed himself for us all."

Annie comes running out of the house. She jumps into my arms and kisses me deeply. "I'm so sorry, Daddy. Please forgive me. It's you I truly love. It always has been."

"I love you, too. I knew it couldn't be true; you wouldn't betray me."

Cletus sheepishly clears his throat. "So, Jack, I was thinking. Mike and Gangus are still gone."

"Yes." I hang my head. "We lost two great men and we will remember them forever."

Cletus shakes his head. "No, Jack, that's not what I mean."

"Well, what are you trying to say, Cletus?"

"Well, I want you to take both Mike and Gangus' arrows and shoot them both at me at the same time."

I look at him like he had grown a second head. "Nope, hell no. Fuck that, Cletus, no fucking way is that happening."

Cletus says, "Jack, please. The people of Immensity need those two brave men more than they need me. Plus, Jack, this time around, I'd be dying a hero and not a slave!"

Annie and I are in tears. "Are you sure, Cletus? Your soul will be split in half and will never be able to come back as a whole."

Cletus smiles, sure of himself. "I have never been surer of anything in my life, Jack."

I pick up the bow; Annie hands me the two arrows.

Cletus sighs. "It's been an honor, Jack. I'm ready when you are."

I shake and cry as I draw the bow back and release the two arrows. They both hit Cletus, one in the chest and the other in the thigh.

Cletus shouts, "Thank you, Jack!"

Cletus's body turns limps and hits the ground. Purple smoke enters both arrows as black smoke releases out of them. The smoke clears to reveal Mike and Gangus.

"You guys!" Annie yells.

"Welcome back!" I hug them both. I pick up the two arrows and Annie grabs Tim's bow. "Let's go back to Immensity; we have a story to tell the people. I'll fill you in on everything on the drive back." We meet Tammy and Raul at the vehicles and all drive back to Immensity.

Gangus and I pull over. We tell the others to keep driving to Immensity. "Gangus and I need to talk really quick."

Mike, Annie, Tammy, and Raul all continue to Immensity.

"Okay, Gangus. So, I found a small chunk of palliridium at Tim's. I made three rings out of it. I want to put the circle together one last time and send the rings to China, to Ya's husband and two children, so that when they die on Earth, they can be reunited with Ya."

Gangus shakes his head. "This doesn't sound like the greatest idea ever, Jack, but I will agree only if we destroy the circle after. We should send a note with the rings so it's not so confusing to Ya's family."

We bond the circle for the last time. I throw the rings and note into the portal. Then, we break the circle, get in the car, and start driving to Immensity. As soon as we get to the Hall, I ring the emergency horn to call a city meeting.

After everyone shows up, I tell the people everything: from the beginning of Tim to the end of Tim. "Clearly, the mission to Earth is no longer happening. We will all stay here and live our lives here. The portal is closed for good.

"Our friend, Cletus, made the ultimate sacrifice for two of our other heroes, Mike and Gangus. Therefore, I declare Cletus' home to be a historic museum showcasing the history of Pluto and the events leading up to Cletus' sacrifice, in case we ever let more people come to this utopia."

The true history is all around them: Cletus' real arrows are hanging above Mike and Gangus' beds; Annie has a replica of Tim's arrow on her desk in our new house. As for the real arrow that holds Tim's soul...well, we agreed to keep that our only secret.

In honor of Cletus, I change the name of Immensity Hall to Two Arrows Hall. Gangus and I agree to take the

Immortal Circle of Life, break it into pieces, and make rings out of it, so every single person of Pluto has a say on whether the portal reopens. Everyone will have to agree and rebound their rings to make the circle whole if they need the portal to open.

I continue to the crowd, "We all have a small Immortal Circle of Life that we can wear proudly; both edges of the rings are red and blue. Above the door of Two Arrows Hall, we will have large replicas of Cletus' two arrows in an X-formation with a big ring binding the arrows together at the middle of the X. There will be a new scroll above the X that says, 'Thank you, Cletus'; below the X, it will say, 'Died a hero, not a slave'."

Chapter 9

In China, Ya's husband, Jing, is now in his early sixties. He stands in the kitchen, cooking a delicious meal for himself and his daughters, Sie and Zen. Jing invited them over for dinner; it's Sie's birthday.

Sie is the youngest; she turns 37 this year. Jing is preparing Kobe beef steaks with sticky rice, vegetables with wasabi sauce, and, of course, his homemade sake. Jing hears a strange noise and sees a bright blue-purple flash of light coming from the living room. He grabs his .38 revolver and heads towards the living room.

Jing looks around with his gun pointing out. He sees nobody, not even any type of damage. Jing looks down and sees three rings and an envelope. Jing sets down the gun on the coffee table next to the envelope. He's unsure if he should open it; maybe he will just wait until the girls get here. Jing decides to wait, so he goes back to the kitchen to finish cooking.

The girls arrive and walk in. Sie says, "Dad, you home?"

"In the kitchen! The food is about done. Just come sit down at the table."

Sie and Zen walk to the table and sit down. Jing brings out a bottle of his sake and three glasses. "Here, girls, pour us all a drink! The food will be a couple more minutes."

Zen grabs the bottle and fills the three glasses. "Happy birthday, little sister," she says as she lifts her glass.

"Thank you, Zen. Cheers!"

Jing brings out three plates and hands the girls their plates. They all eat their tender, medium-rare Kobe steaks. "So, Dad," Zen says. "I couldn't help but notice when we walked in that your gun is sitting on the table. What have you got yourself into now?"

Jing replies, "Oh, I almost forgot about that. That's nothing. This strange envelope and a few rings appeared out of the blue. I was waiting for you two to get here to open it."

Sie replies, "I told you, Dad, not to get me anything for my birthday."

Jing laughs. "No, Sie, you're eating your present. Like I said, that envelope just appeared here a few minutes before you two got here."

Zen runs to the living room. "Why are we sitting here? Let's go open it and see what it says!"

Jing and Sie follow Zen into the living room. Jing sits down on the couch; his daughters sit down next to him, one on each side, as Jing reaches for the envelope. He says, "Maybe we shouldn't open it; we don't know where it came from or who it's from. I mean, envelopes don't just appear out of thin air. These rings are very strange looking. One side is red and the other is blue. What type of material are these made of?"

Zen and Sie roll their eyes. Zen excitedly says, "Dad, come on, just open it!"

Sie agrees. "Yeah, just open it."

Jing opens the envelope slowly and takes out a letter. He starts to read it out loud. "The letter says 'Dear Jing, Zen. and Sie, this letter and these rings may come as a shock to you. Please take the time to read the whole thing. My name is Jack. This letter and these rings came from the city of Immensity on the planet Pluto. This is where Ya is now living an immortal life. Yes, Ya, Jing. Your wife. Zen and Sie, your mother."

All three of them are crying. Jing stops reading, stands up, and walks around, trying to gather himself. He grabs his bottle of sake and the glasses. While Jing is out of the room, Zen and Sie look at each other. "Do you believe this, Zen?"

"I'm just waiting for the rest of it; then I'll determine if I believe it or not."

Jing returns to the couch with his sake and glasses takes a big drink. He continues to read where he left off.

"I know this all sounds crazy, but if you look in the envelope, there are two pictures: one of Ya at her new home and another of her in front of the building she constructed as the head architect."

Zen reaches in the envelope, pulls out the pictures, and starts crying. She looks at Jing and says, "It's her, Dad! It's really her."

"And the building?" asks Jing.

Zen hands him the building picture. Jing is shocked. He replies, "It's her. Look, she did it!" He proudly waves the picture in his daughters' faces. "She built the building we drew up together."

Jing continues to read: "So, hopefully, these pictures are enough proof that you believe this letter. I will not go into great detail, but I will tell you that when the three of you die, as long as you have one of the rings on you, you will come here and be reunited with Ya. The only rule is that you cannot kill yourselves to get here. The rings are made of palliridium, a very rare metal only found on Pluto, or as we call it, Earth Two. Each of you, take a ring and don't lose it. I'm putting my full trust in you three. Ya doesn't know I did this for her, so it will come as a surprise when you get here. I am awaiting your arrival.

Until we meet,

Jack."

Jing, Zen, and Sie all reach out and grab a ring. Zen puts it on her right pinky; Sie puts it on her big toe so that it won't be stolen; Jing takes off his necklace, slides the ring on it, and puts it back on.

Jing says, "Well, Sie, it wasn't planned, but how about that as a birthday present?" He laughs though his tears.

She smiles at him. "Yes, Dad, this is the greatest present ever, knowing when I die, I get to finally see Mom and be able to remember it."

"Yes, you both were so young when she was taken away from us. Thankfully, Sie, you came back to find me and your sister when you became an adult."

The two girls give Jing kisses on the forehead and leave to go back home. "Thanks for the meal, Dad." Sie hugs and kisses her father again.

"Yes, it was delicious!" Zen agrees. "Bye, Dad. Love you."

"I love you both, too. Drive safely."

Jing gets up, still shocked. He grabs his necklace, looks at his ring, kisses it, and walks toward his bedroom to go to sleep.

Zen and Sie ride back home together. Zen is driving.

At a stoplight, Zen, a little drunk, runs the red light, smashing into the side of a semi-truck trailer. The car's roof peels back like a can of sardines. Both girls are decapitated, as if the truck turned into a guillotine, from the force of hitting and sliding under the trailer.

Rescue units, cops, and the coroner show up. The coroner bags up the girls and brings them to the morgue.

Jing get a knock on his door. He opens it and is greeted by a couple of police officers. "Can I help you, officers?"

The officers both have solemn looks on their faces. "Sir, can we come in? You might want to have a seat."

The officers explain the accident and that both of Jing's daughters have died.

"No, no, no, they were just here! It was my baby's birthday! Tell me it's not true." Jing drops to floor, crying and punching the floor.

"We are really sorry for your loss, sir. We will leave our card on the table. Have a good night; again, very sorry." As the officers are walking out, one officer says to the other, "I mean, if he was any kind of father, he wouldn't have let them drive home drunk." The officer shuts the door, not realizing that Jing heard every word.

Meanwhile, on Pluto, I'm at Gangus' house having a beer. "You feel that?" I ask him; there's a low hum in the atmosphere, and I feel a strange presence wash over me.

Gangus replies, "Feel what, Jack?"

"I just have a strange feeling over me, like a strange presence or something."

"Oh, that? I just thought maybe I was drunk," he says with a laugh.

I ignore his comment. "Gangus, when the portal opens, where does it open to?"

"The same place that you put the circle together. Why, Jack?"

"Come, Gangus. We need to go look."

"Really, Jack? It's only been a year; it's way too soon."

I shake my head defiantly. "Nope. Let's go, Gangus."

We leave and go to where we bonded the Immortal Circle of Life outside of the city. As we drive there, Gangus sees a yellow haze ahead. He looks at me and says, "Jack, that yellow haze means the portal was opened!"

"Well, I'm not sure what to expect, but it's got to be one of Ya's family members."

Gangus stops the truck. We hop out, both grabbing a HSF100 gun from the box of the truck and approach on foot. As the yellow haze start to lift, we see two figures ahead. We can hear muffled voices; it appears to be two ladies talking.

"Gangus," I say, "it must be Zen and Sie, Ya's daughters."

Gangus replies, "Let's hope so! Zen, Sie, is that you?"

We hear someone reply, "Yes, it's us! Who are you? Where are we? What happened?"

I start running toward the sisters, yelling, "Stay there; I'm coming!"

We finally reach the sisters. "Hello, Zen and Sie. I'm Jack, and this is Gangus."

Zen replies, "Like Jack from the letter? Is this Earth Two?"

I nod. "Yes, it is. Come with us; we will bring you to Immensity to your mother's place."

Jing now lives all alone. Depression has begun to sink in. He has to figure out a way to afford two funerals for his daughters. He thinks to himself, "I have this ring. I'm sure someone would pay a lot of money for it."

Jing starts looking around on the dark web. He sees a lot of human organ ads: "Sell your kidney! You only need one!" Jing didn't want to do anything like that but thought maybe they might know who to talk to about this ring. Jing e-mails them.

In a matter of a few minutes, Jing gets an e-mail back with a dark web website link. Jing clicks the link; it brings him to a page for a self-proclaimed mad scientist that wants to take over the world. His name is Lars; he's from Iceland.

Jing e-mails Lars and tells him he has a rare ring made of palliridium from Pluto and a letter of proof. Within a few minutes, he receives a reply. It says, "Jing, if what you have is real, you just became a rich man. I went ahead a booked you a flight on a private jet to my laboratory in Iceland. Get to the airport ASAP; remember the ring and letter. When my driver picks you up at the airport, he will bring you to me. Here is the password to get in. See you soon."

Jing knows that what he is about to do is wrong, but he has no other choice. He heard what the officer said; he thinks his daughters and wife probably won't want to see him anyway.

Jing packs a bag and heads to the airport.

Back on Pluto, Gangus and I bring Zen and Sie to Ya's. We knock on the door; Ya says, "Come in."

We enter. "Ya," I say, "you have done so much for this city. I cannot begin to explain how thankful I am. Your story still pulls on my heart strings. That being said, hopefully you're not mad, but sit down; I have a surprise for you." I walk to the door and wave for Zen and Sie to come in. They nervously walk to the door and come inside.

Ya looks at them both and looks at me. "How did you do this, Jack? Is that really my girls?" Ya, in tears, runs to them. They all hug each other.

"I will explain later, Ya. You three have a lot of catching up to do."

As Gangus and I leave, all three of the ladies thank us.

I say softly, "You're more than welcome. Thank you, Ya." I shut the door.

On Earth, Jing makes it to Iceland. He is riding in the back of a limousine. His driver pulls up to a huge iron gate with a speaker and camera near it. Jing pushes the call button.

A gruff voice comes over the speaker. "Who's there? What's the password?"

Jing meekly replies, "It's Jing. Umm, password is 'Green Monkeys Fly at Midnight'."

"You may enter." The gate opens.

Jing gets out of the limo and walks through the gate. He sees a door on this vast, flat, white building. A man, one that Jing assumes is Lars, walks out the door, "You must be Jing," he says, holding out his hand.

Jing shakes the man's hand. "And you must be Lars."

The man nods. "Well, welcome to my lab. Let's go inside so I can look at this ring and letter." Lars and Jing walk inside. "Would you like anything to drink or eat, Jing? Maybe some alcohol?"

Jing perks up at the mention of alcohol. "Maybe an alcoholic drink; that sounds nice."

Lars chuckles. "Of course, of course! The bar is through this door; let's go sit and have a few drinks."

Lars and Jing sit down; a topless waitress takes their order. Lars eyes her and then brings his attention back around to the man sitting next to him. "So, Jing, can I see the ring and letter?"

"Of course." Jing pulls out the ring and letter and hands them to Lars. Lars opens the letter and starts to read it.

The waitress comes with their drinks. "Here you go, gentlemen."

Jing can't help but stare at the waitress' breasts jiggle with every move she makes. He manages to stutter out, "Th-thank you, mi-miss."

"Jing," Lars says, "Do you have the two pictures as well?"

"Yes, I do." Tears form in Jing's eyes. "Could I keep them, though? It will be the only thing I have left of her."

Lars smiles. "The photos are of your wife? Yes, of course. I will just scan them to my computer; then, you may keep them." Lars looks at the ring as he finishes reading the letter. "This place sounds amazing. Why would you want to sell this ring?"

Jing explains his struggles with bills. He tells Lars about his daughters' deaths, his health issues, everything.

Lars shakes his head. "Wow, sorry to hear that. Well, everything looks good and appears to be the real deal. Do you mind if I try a test on this ring?"

Jing says, "Go ahead, but if you break it, you just bought it for my price."

Lars chuckles. "Of course. Sounds like a deal. Wait here, Jing. I'll be back after the test is done. In the meantime, have some more drinks, or have Helen entertain you with those tits!"

Lars grabs the ring and brings it to the lab. Lars tries to drill it, but every bit he tries on it breaks. He tries dropping acids on it, but they just run off it. He tries to freeze it: nothing. He tries to melt it: still nothing. "Nothing is effective," Lars says. "This has to be the real deal."

Lars grabs the ring and heads back to the bar. He walks in the bar and is greeted by Jing sucking on Helen's nipples and Helen giving Jing a hand job. "Oh! Sorry, am I interrupting something?" Lars laughs.

Jing quickly stuffs his cock back in his pants, embarrassed. He stumbles over his words. "No, no, no! We were just...umm...passing the time as we waited for you, Lars."

Lars laughs. "Well, you didn't need to stop on my account. But this ring, Jing! I want it. How much?" Lars asks.

"Well, it's rare. It's not from Earth, and since my girls are gone, it's now one of a kind on Earth, too. I don't really know how to put a price tag on something like this." Jing shrugs his shoulders in confusion and takes a gulp from his drink.

Lars smiles. "How does 700 million sound to you, Jing?"

Jing spits out his drink. "W-well, I...umm...I—"

"No? How about 900 million?"

Jing shouts, "Yes! Yes, that's perfect!" The two shake hands.

"I'll go scan these pictures and wire 899 million to your account. When I bring you the pictures back, I'll have one million in cash.

Jing says, "Yes, sounds good."

Lars grabs the ring and pictures. "Helen, finish him off, please," Lars says as he walks out the door.

Jing, very happy with the deal, sees Helen walking back toward him. Jing whips out his cock excitedly. Helen saunters over to Jing, pulls out a knife, and slits his throat.

Chapter 10

Lars wakes up in a mysterious place. "Where am I?" he thinks to himself. "I don't even remember going to sleep! Last thing I remember was grabbing the ring and pictures and heading to the lab. I remember telling Helen to finish him off."

He laughs and says out loud, "Oh, shit! She probably thought I meant to kill him. I meant making him cum." He laughs again. "Oh, well, I got the ring for free!"

He looks around, taking in his surroundings. This place looks nothing like Iceland. "This must be Earth Two. If Helen *did* kill Jing, then I would have been holding the ring when he died. I need to find this city, Immensity." Lars starts walking.

In the city, Ya and her daughters have some drinks. Zen and Sie want to learn more about this place.

"Well," Ya says, "tomorrow we can go to Cletus' museum. You will find everything you want to know there."

Zen asks, "So, are there any handsome men here?"

Sie giggles. "Yeah, Mom! Where's the men at?" Sie says.

Ya rolls her eyes. "Well, girls, there are lots of men here. The only ones I know of that are unavailable are Jack and Raul. Jack is with Annie and Raul is with Tammy. Besides them, it's like a buffet!"

All three ladies laugh.

"Okay, girls. We should probably get some sleep; it will be a long day tomorrow, learning about this place."

Mike is over at our place, talking to me. Mike says, "Jack, can I ask you something? I was thinking about something. I'm getting bored of the city, and I know we built up Immensity and have everything anyone needs, but I'm a country boy. There is a lot of land outside the city. Could I just move out to the country and start a ranch or something?"

"Mike," I say, "I'm a country boy, too, and I completely understand wanting to move out of the city. You know I would do anything for you, but you also know how we run Immensity. We can bring it up in the weekly meeting. Everyone will vote, all 49,996; well, now 49,998. If you get 35,000 votes 'Yes', you can move to the country."

Mike replies, "Okay, sweet! Thanks, Jack. Wait, 49,998 people? When did we gain two people? And how did we gain two people?"

I smile and shake my head. "It was something Gangus and I agreed on. They got here today: Zen and Sie. They are Ya's daughters."

"Oh, that's cool. Ya deserves that. Are they hot? I could go for some freak-ass Chinese pussy."

I bellow. "Get out of here, Mike! Go find out yourself."

Mike gives me a cheesy grin. "Alright, Jack, see you later, and thanks again."

"Of course, anything for you, bro. Oh, Mike?"

Mike turns around. "Yeah?"

"To answer your question: yes, they are hot, by the way."

Mike chuckles. "Okay, thanks for the heads-up; I'll check them out tomorrow. Good night, Jack."

I wave at him. "Good night, Mike."

Lars has been walking for hours. Finally, he sees what looks like buildings up ahead. He thinks to himself, "Finally." He gets closer and closer. "What kind of city doesn't have lights?"

He looks around a little more, taking in the environment. He sees buildings that seem to be in a triangle formation. "This place isn't so great," he mutters. He gets to the garage door, which is hanging open, and walks through. He walks up the stairs that come out to a courtyard.

Lars sees a house in the middle of the three buildings. He walks up to the door and knocks. "Hello? Hello, anybody home?"

He walks around the house, looking around: nobody. He continues to the second floor and looks in every room. There is nobody here.

Lars noticed a broken window in the room where he is now. "Wow, what happened here? Why is there nobody here? I'll need to look more in the morning; I need some sleep."

Lars lays down in the unmade bed and goes to sleep.

Mike wakes up and heads towards Ya's place to introduce himself to Ya's hot daughters, Zen and Sie.

I wake up, remembering to put Mike's request to live in the country on the weekly meeting agenda.

Lars wakes up to start looking around for clues as to why nobody is here.

Ya wakes her girls up so they can start their day. Ya hears a knock on the door. "Who is it?" she shouts.

"It's Mike, Ya!"

"Come in, Mike."

Mike walks in. "Good morning, Ya."

Ya replies, "Good morning, Mike. I was just getting ready to cook some breakfast. You want some?"

"Well, sure, I can't turn down your delicious cooking!"

Ya smiles. "What brings you by my place so early today?"

Mike says, "Well, I was over at Jack's last night and he mentioned your daughters are here now."

Ya gives Mike a suspicious smirk. "Yes, they are. We are going to Cletus' today; they want to learn about Immensity."

"Well, that's a very good way to learn. Mind if I tag along?"

Ya looks at Mike sideways. "I know what you're up to, Mike."

He chuckles. "No, Ya, I just want to come with you in case they have questions. I mean, Cletus *did* save me and Gangus."

"Okay, fine."

Mike gets excited to see what Zen and Sie look like. Zen walks out the den, half-naked in her bra and panties. She sees Mike eyeballing her up and down. Embarrassed, she tries to cover herself up. "Mom! Why didn't you tell us we had company?"

Ya pokes her head around the corner and eyes her daughter. "Well, why are you walking around like that? Go! Go get some clothes on."

Zen runs into the den, red and embarrassed.

Sie, lounging in a cozy papasan, asks, "What's wrong with you?"

Zen replies, "Mom didn't say we had company. I was just going to the bathroom, thinking it was just us here! Otherwise, I would have at least put my robe on."

Sie giggles. "Well, who is it?"

"I don't know his name, but he was looking me up and down like I was his breakfast."

Sie giggles louder. "Well, maybe you should be; he wants some of that ass! So, is he cute?"

"Oh, my, Sie! Let me tell you: he is a gorgeous piece of man."

Ya yells out, "Girls, come on! Breakfast is ready." She laughs and adds, "Oh, yeah, and we have company!"

Meanwhile, on the other side, Lars finds what looks like blueprints to a city; they are drawn from a bird's eye view. He sees the triangle buildings and the house he is in now, but they're labeled 'Tim's place'. Nowhere does it say 'Immensity'. Lars thinks to himself, "Well, were there two cities? Who is Tim?"

Looking more into the overhead drawings, he notices more buildings, labeled 'factories' and 'warehouses'. One of them say 'factory/mine'.

Ya, Zen, Sie, and Mike finish up breakfast and head out to the museum.

"Zen," Mike says. "You want to ride with me?"

Sie giggles as she says under her breath, "That's not the kind of ride she wants."

Zen nudges Sie with her elbow sharply, blushing. "Shut up, Sie! Yes, Mike, I would love that. Thank you."

Sie sarcastically says, "Hey, now! Get it on!"

"Girls!" Ya shouts. "Get your pussies under control."

Mike's face turns blood red; he hangs his head down in disbelief that Ya just said that out loud. He thinks to himself, "It's only a matter of time before I'm sliding into Zen!"

Ya and Sie get in Ya's car. Mike and Zen get into Mike's truck. The four of them drive to the museum.

On the other side, Lars looks through every drawer and any possible hiding spot throughout the house, searching for clues as to who Tim is. He's not having any luck, so far.

He walks into the den and sees a bookshelf. He takes books off one at a time, flipping through pages, looking for any loose articles that may have been put in a book.

As he grabs one after the other, he gets to one that feels different than the rest. When he tries to pull it off the shelf, the bookcase starts to lift into the ceiling. "Whoever this Tim guy is," he thinks to himself, "I like his style. A hidden room!" Lars walks inside.

Chapter 11

Ya, Sie, Zen, and Mike walk around the museum for hours, reading and watching videos on the history of Immensity and Earth Two. Zen reads about Mike's bravery. She takes Mike by the hand and looks deep in his eyes.

"Wow, you are a brave man. Did you really jump in front of that arrow to save Cletus?"

Mike blushes. "Yes, everything you have seen here or read is all true, Zen." Now, more than ever, she feels the butterflies in her stomach for this man.

"Wow, so you saved Cletus, and then Cletus saved you and Gangus. That's true heroic shit right there."

Mike smiles. "Well, ladies, now that you know the history of this place, could I offer you ladies a ride back to my place for steaks, beer, wine, and good conversation?" All three agree.

Lars walks into the hidden room and sees a desk and what appears to be a bow. There is also an all-access badge and a letter. Lars grabs the badge and sticks it in his back pocket. He then grabs the letter, sits down, and starts to read it:

Dear whoever has found this,

If you're reading this, that means I'm gone. My name is Tim. I was one of the Overseers here, as is Gangus. I went

ahead and made an exact replica of my bow. The one half of
the Immortal Circle of Life bow I once had, but this bow can
both take souls and do reverse-soul exchange. Again, if
you're reading this, that means I'm gone. My soul is trapped
in a arrow. All you need to do is find this arrow, shoot it with
the bow on the desk at anybody in Immensity, and the soul
exchange will happen. I can explain everything else then.

Lars shakes his head in complete confusion. He assumed Tim was an evil guy like himself. Now he knows he needs to find this arrow. Lars grabs the bow and leaves the room. He knows he needs to find the arrow but wants to see what the badge is all about.

Meanwhile, at Mike's, Ya, Sie, Zen, and Mike finish up eating dinner. They all sit around, drinking, joking, talking. Ya stands up and says, "Well, look at the time! We should really be on our way, girls."

"So soon?" Mike frowns. "No, stay a while longer! I'm enjoying this."

Ya graciously declines. "Sorry, Mike! Maybe another time; we have the city meeting tomorrow."

Mike says, "Yeah, I understand. Remember to vote yes for my proposal!"

Ya laughs. "Of course, I will. Girls, you ready?"

Sie stands up. "Yes, Mom, I'm ready."

Zen is a little more hesitant. "I just kind of want to stay here, if that's okay with Mike." She looks over at him.

Mike looks at Zen, surprised. He says, "Well, of course that's okay with me. I can drive you home later, or I've got an extra room you could crash in."

Ya rolls her eyes. "Oh, okay, well have fun, you two. Let's go, Sie."

As Sie and Ya walk out the door, Sie giggles, looks at her sister, and says, "Bowchickawawa!" as she thrusts the air and closes the door.

Zen, blushing, says, "Oh my god, I'm so sorry. You have to excuse my little sister. Her mind is always in the gutter; she turns everything sexual."

"No need to apologize, beautiful."

Lars takes another look at the overhead drawing he found. He decides to go and look around this factory, mine building, whatever it was. He starts walking and gets to what he believes is the building he's looking for. He tries to open the door; it's locked. Lars sees a scanner next to the door. He reaches in his back pocket, pulls out the badge, and tries to scan it.

Lars hears the door unlock and opens it. All the lights come on. "Welcome, Tim" over the speakers. "Oh, yeah," he says, "this Tim guy was evil."

Lars walks through the factory. He sees nothing but huge containers of a blueish-silver material. He pulls out the ring he has in his pocket. "Holy shit, is this all palliridium, like this ring?"

Lars sees a door towards the back of the factory and starts walking towards it. He passes through hundreds of these containers, all filled with what he thinks is palliridium. He opens the door with the badge and, again, all the lights come on. Again, he hears the voice. "Welcome, Tim. Would you like to start the dredge?"

Lars doesn't reply; he knows it's probably only programmed to Tim's voice. He walks in a little bit further and sees huge buckets, one after another, going down a huge, deep hole. "So, this is a mine and these buckets are the dredge," he thinks to himself. "This all must be palliridium. I really need to find this arrow. Tomorrow, I will travel to Immensity. The letter said it was on the other side. I wonder if this badge will start any of the vehicles in the garage."

He heads back to the house to get some sleep.

The next morning, on the other side, everyone is gathered at Two Arrows Hall for the weekly meeting. Mike says to Zen, "Let's go pick up your mom and sister. I'm sure Jack will have you backstage to introduce yourself and Sie."

He kisses her cheek. "I must say, Zen, some of the things you did last night...wow! Like porn star shit; it was amazing."

Zen giggles. "Well, I'm glad you enjoyed it; I know I did."

They hop in the truck and drive to Ya's place.

On the other side, Lars is trying to figure out what vehicles this badge might start. He walks up to a very sporty-looking car, thinking it will be fast. He holds the badge up by the door handle. It unlocks and starts up. He knows by the sound of the car that he chose the right one.

He gets in and hears a voice. "What's your destination?"

Lars replies, "Immensity."

"Any particular address or just to the center of the city?"

"The center of the city is fine."

"Confirmed. Destination: Two Arrows Hall. You should be at Two Arrows Hall in 25 minutes. Sit back and enjoy your ride."

There are cold beverages in the center console. The car takes off driving on its own. Lars thinks to himself, "This is the shit I'm talking about right here." He opens the center console, grabs a bottle of beer, and kicks back.

In Immensity, on the other side, Mike picks up Ya and Sie. They meet me backstage. I say, "Good to see everyone.

Mike, your proposal is last. Me and Gangus will tell everyone what we agreed on about Jing, Zen, and Sie, and then introduce them to everyone. We will tell them that this is the last secret Immensity will ever have, besides the mystery of where Tim's arrow is. At that point, Gangus will let everyone know what we did with it; then, there will be no more secrets."

Mike says, "Sure, get everyone in an uproar before hearing my proposal!" He chuckles.

Lars arrives at Two Arrows Hall, gets out of the car, and follows the crowd of people entering the Hall.

Gangus and I are centerstage. "Welcome, everyone!" I wave at the crowd. "This should be the most exciting meeting we have had yet, at least in my eyes and, hopefully, yours as well. Back a year ago, when we defeated Tim, Gangus and I agreed to bond the Immortal Circle of Life one last time. We threw three rings, the same rings we all have today in the portal, knowing it would take about a year to get to Earth. We all know who Ya is and we all know her story. Well, those three rings went to her husband and two daughters.

"About two or three days ago, Ya's daughters, Zen and Sie, made it here. I would like to introduce them to you all; everyone welcome Zen and Sie!"

114

Mike gives Zen a kiss. "Your big moment, baby! Have fun. Be great!" he shouts as he slaps her on the ass.

Sie says, "Oh, so you guys did it, huh?" She giggles.

Both girls walk out on stage. The people of Immensity give the girls a standing round of applause. The echoes of welcomes run through the Hall. Lars takes this information in.

As the applause dies down, I say, "Okay, now we, as the people of Immensity, have welcomed them. Now, we need to build them houses and have them pick out their vehicles. So, everyone, that's the last secret of Immensity, except for the location of Tim's arrow."

Gangus stands up. The anticipation killing Lars, but finally he will find out where this arrow is.

"People of Immensity," Gangus booms. "This is the very last secret. There are no more and will never be another ever again. Alright everyone, we hid the arrow in the same place I hid my piece of the Immortal Circle of Life for 38 years. Nobody found it, so I figured it was safe enough to hide the arrow.

"Halfway between here and Tim's is a cave, where Tim and I met every year to open the portal. Only my key and Tim's key will open the cave. We still haven't found Tim's key, so I ask you all now, especially the people that worked for Tim: if you have or know where his key is, please turn it in to me so we can destroy it. That way, no evil will ever come to Earth Two."

The people of Immensity erupt with cheers. Lars sits back, thinking, "I was right! Tim was evil and now I know where his arrow is. I wonder if this badge thing is what they meant by 'key'. It almost has to be. I have to find this cave."

He gets up and leaves the hall.

"Okay, everyone," I say. "Thank you, Gangus. Now, the last order of business. We all know Mike and his heroism with saving Cletus. He would like to come forth and propose something. Mike?" I gesture at Mike with the microphone.

Mike steps up beside me. "Thank you, everyone, for your time to hear my proposal. I would like to move outside of Immensity to the country and start a ranch with some cattle and deer. I want to open a hunting preserve. I wouldn't be too far outside the city, maybe between two and five miles, but in order for me to have a ranch, hunting preserve, and reservation, where you're all welcome to come hunt, I'd need 500 acres of land. So that's my proposal; thank you all again for your time."

The people clap loudly for Mike.

I take the microphone back from him. "Alright, people of Immensity, it's time to vote. If you want Mike to be able to move, pick up the controller under your seat and press the red button. If you don't want him to move, hit the blue button on the controller. Mike needs 35,000 or more to move."

The votes start coming in on the overhead Jumbotron. In a matter of a few minutes, the votes are in: 37,567 for yes, 12,431 for no. Mike jumps for joy, looks at Zen, and says, "Would you like to live there with me?"

Zen replies, giggling like a schoolgirl, "Yes, of course!"

"Well," I say, "looks like Mike will get his ranch and hunting preserve. That's all for this meeting. Thank you, everyone! Let's go and get started building Zen and Sie their new homes and help Mike build his."

Mike says, "Wait, Jack! One last thing. Everyone, thank you all so much for letting me do this. Our work just got easier: Zen has agreed to live with me on the ranch, so we only need to build the ranch and Sie's house, now."

"Great!" I clap my hands. "Thank you all for coming. Have a safe and enjoyable rest of your day."

I look at Mike. "You sly dog! how was that pussy, huh?"

Mike laughs. "Absolutely amazing."

"Well, let's go look for your 500 acres."

Chapter 12

Lars sits in the car outside Two Arrows Hall waiting for the crowd to leave. He picks what seems to be a weak subject to kidnap and take with him to the cave. He desperately hopes that the badge he has is really Tim's key. If it is, he can perform the reverse-soul exchange in the cave. That way, if Gangus ever checks, there is an arrow still there.

Mike and Zen meet up with me and Annie outside the hall. Mike says, "Hop in; let's go look for the perfect place for the ranch."

We get into Mike's truck and start heading out of town.

Most of the people of Immensity have left the Hall; there are only a few left outside chatting. Lars zones in on a target: an older, skinny, frail man, probably in his late sixties. Flipping through the GPS, in the saved destinations, Lars finds a destination: "Cave."

Lars pulls up to the older man. "Hey, buddy, need a ride?"

The guy says, "Sure, I appreciate that. Thank you."

The man sits in the seat and shuts the car door. Lars opens the center console and asks the guy if he wants a beer. The guy nods.

Lars pulls out a beer and hits the guy in the head with the bottle, knocking the man out cold, and starts the GPS navigation for the cave. A voice comes on. "Auto-pilot or manual drive?"

Lars answers, "Auto, and hurry!"

The voice says, "Destination: cave. You should reach Cave in 10 to 12 minutes." The car takes off. Lars looks around for anything to tie the man up with. He can't find anything.

Ya and Sie are out looking for a vehicle for Sie. Ya asks Sie, "What do you want: car, truck, SUV?"

Sie says, "I don't know. I don't have any money."

Ya laughs. "You don't need money; you just pick one and then it's yours."

Sie pick out a little sports car. "Meet you at home, Mom!" She takes off.

Ya waves back, laughing. "Okay, drive safe!"

Mike and the others are about 3 miles out of Immensity when Mike stops the truck. He thinks he has found the perfect piece of land for the ranch. Mike, Zen, Annie, and I get out of the truck.

Mike starts walking around. "See, we could put the house here and fence in 200 acres behind it for the cattle. Over there, with the woods, open pasture, pond, and creek: fence that 280 acres in for the hunting preserve. We could keep 20 acres not fenced for our yard and whatever else we want."

Zen looks around as Mike is describing everything and says, "Yes, this is perfect. We could put a garden over here and fruit orchards over there. This is truly a perfect place; I love it."

I reply. "Well, it's settled then. This will be your new home!"

Annie smiles. "This calls for a celebration drink."

Everyone cheers in agreement.

Ya and Sie get back to Ya's place. Sitting in the living room, Sie says, "Mom? Don't you think Zen moving in with Mike is rather fast?"

Ya smiles and shrugs her shoulders. "Yes, kind of, but Mike is a very handsome man. He is like Jack's best friend, so he's higher up on the ladder then most of the people of Immensity."

"Exactly. That's what I don't understand. The people of Immensity all vote on everything and they say everyone has a say, so why do Jack and Gangus act like it's their city?"

Ya replies, "You clearly didn't pay attention when we were at Cletus' house, did you? Gangus was an Overseer, who made this city and picked the people to be here. It *is* his city. Gangus picked Jack last to bring the people together, to believe in the same dream as Gangus. He accomplished that, so Jack is Gangus' right-hand man. Mike is Jack's right-hand man and best friend. Why, Sie? Do you not like it here?"

"No, no, it's not that. This place is perfect. I just don't understand the chain of command, I guess."

"Well, don't go pissing off Jack; he is the reason you're here, Sie."

"I know, Mom. I know; just overwhelmed with everything, I guess."

"I understand how that is. Hopefully your house will be done in a few days."

Sie smiles. "Yes, that will be nice. I'm excited. So, Mom, there were over 14,000 people that voted no for Mike not to move. Is there a way to find out who those people are?"

Ya thinks for a minute. "I don't know. Why would you want to know that?"

Sie replies, "Oh, nothing. I was just wondering."

Lars gets to the cave and tries scanning the key. To his surprise, the cave opens. "It worked! Holy shit, it actually worked."

Lars sits the man against the wall in the inside of the cave. Looking around for the arrow, he finally finds it, draws the arrow back, and releases the arrow, hitting the man in the chest. His body goes limp, falling to the cave floor. Lars sees a black smoke being sucked into the arrow. The arrow itself releases a purplish smoke.

Lars' mouth hangs open, amazed at what he is seeing. "It's really working!" Lars shouts to himself as the black and purple smoke clears. Lars sees a man sitting against the wall, not the same man he brought in here. "Hello, are you Tim?"

The man looks around, disoriented. He rubs his eyes and stretches before reaching his hand out to Lars. "Yes, and you are?"